# THE BATTLE FOR THE ALAMO TAQUERIA

by
Nick Iuppa & John Pesqueira

Cover designed by David Pettigrew
Cover photo: © 2016
Published by Dos Milagros Press
Visit the author website: http://www.nickiuppawrites.com

ISBN-13: 978-0-9989806-1-4

10  9  8  7  6  5  4  3  2  1

## Novels by Nick Iuppa
## & John Pesqueira

*THE CARLOS MANN TRILOGY*
*Alicia's Ghost*
*Alicia's Sin*
*Alicia Bewitched*

*Avenging Adelita*
*Esteban's Quest*
*Esteban Meets Alicia*

## Novels by Nick Iuppa

*Taken by Witches*
*The Witch Within Her*

*Bloody Bess and the Doomsday Games*

# Praise for Alicia's Ghost

*"Irresistible characters in a wicked tale of suspense"*
— Suzanna B. Stinnett, Author of *Starship Interlude*

*"Who could have guessed that ghost sex would be so hot?!?! This page-turner had so many twists and turns that my head was spinning."* — Janey Baker, Actress

*"Ghostly fun."*
— Marc Wade, Executive Producer, Digital Media

*"Funny & fun to read! Kept me wondering what would happen next."*
— Eric Dueker, Filmmaker

*"Incredibly imaginative!"* — Chuck Reedy, Author

*"The storytelling is excellent. Can't wait for the sequel."*
— Elke Hitto, Writer/Journalist

*"I love the characters, and Alicia... these guys have the Latina in her down to a science."*
— Becky Escamilla, Constant Reader

*"So intriguing... demands attention."*
— Rick Emond, Graphic Novelist

*"These guys certainly spin a great tale. Hope they keep cranking out stories for readers to enjoy."*
— Dave Couzins, Author of *Domers*

*"If you think you'd like a world where ghosts whip up dim sum and enjoy making love with the living, then this book is for you."*
— Terry Borst, Screenwriter

# Dedication

*For Luis Alberto Urrea for his stories,*
*his inspiration, and his example*


*"I am more interested in bridges, not borders."*
*—Luis Urrea*

# Acknowledgments

We'd like to thank the friends and colleagues who offered valuable advice and help during the creation of this book, especially: Lauren Ayer, Norma Cervantes, D. Thrush, David Pettigrew, Bram Druckman, and Janet Grady. We appreciate the fast, professional, and very competent services we received from our graphic designer, Laurie Douglas. And thanks to Tara McNabb for her fine editorial work.

*I will build a great, great wall on our southern border, and I will make Mexico pay for that wall.*

*I guarantee they will pay for it, and they will be very, very happy about it.*

— US President Donald Trump

# Contents

**PART THREE**

# Characters

## Major Characters

Claudia Madero (Visionary young woman from a small town in Mexico)

Maria Madero (Her practical sister)

Antonio Cervantes (An admirer of Claudia)

Nacho – Francisco Alfredo Gonzales Gonzales Gonzales – (Their friend since childhood)

Clayton Bailey (Texas vigilante who sees himself as The Lone Stranger)

Nick Fleming (Owner of the Eden Mellon Ranch in Texas)

Britney Fleming (Nick's sister, singer in an all girl band)

## Minor Characters

Daniel Drivel (President of the United States)

Appassionata Sanchez (A Spy)

Hector Oliva (Wealthy head of the Mexican Bean Combine aka The King of Beans)

Hector Oliva Junior (the Prince of Beans)

Tío Joaquín (Claudia's Uncle)

Tío Rafael (Joaquin's Brother)

Padre Carlos (Parish Priest)

Manuel Rosas (Owner of the Alamo Taqueria)

Frankie Lopez (Famous Mexican-American Comedian)

Chato (Bully from Maria's childhood who becomes a priest)

Tía Lucinda (Tío Rafael's Wife)

Andy Myers (Side-kick of Clayton Bailey)

Toronto Bailey (Clayton Bailey's nephew, visiting from Canada)

Emilio (Sleazy brother of The King of Beans)

Juanito (Maria's son)

Don Juan Rodriquez (Commander from the Mexican Army who trains Claudia's troops)

Ricardo de la Palma Alta (The President of Mexico)

Renaldo (Cousin of Antonio who tells his story of America)

Morena (Renaldo's wife)

**Others**

Jesus Morales (A Coyote)

Angela, Pepe and 3 men from Vera Cruz (On the march into Texas)

Julio (Forman in the Melon fields)

Lola (Maria's friend in the field)

Kids from Maria's childhood (Ramundo –Little Cousin Veronica)

Old Pedro (crazy old altar boy in Maria's story)

The Mexican Wrestlers (El Leon, Coyote Gordo, Garapata, Gara Nalgas, Pepito El Bonito)

Nancy Malone and her son Johnny (Witnesses to Nacho's beating)

Doctor Johnson (Nacho's doctor at the hospital)

Rosie Alvarez (Newspaper reporter who discovers Claudia)

Gerald (the President's aid)

Miguel (Assistant to The King of Beans)

Salvador and Fabiola Rosas, (Founders of the Alamo Taqueria)

Emma Rosas (Daughter at the Alamo Taqueria)

Linda Rhinestone (Cashier at the Alamo Gift Shop)

Wayne Duke (Star of the film The Alamo)

Chuck Hardesty (Marine Commander at the Alamo Taqueria)

General Bradley Oldman (US Commander at the border)

Mona Esposito (his aid)

Ginger Mccloskey (A reporter at the Alamo Taqueria)

Wolfe Trapp (Anchorman at CNN)

General Suárez (commander of the Mexican Army at the border)

Bobby Joe Connelly (Malevolent-looking, anti-immigration senator)

# Part One

# Chapter One

Claudia knows that she's just made the worst mistake of her life.

Stretching out before her is a seemingly endless vista of desert, dark, rugged mountains, and hardpan interrupted only by low twisted trees.

Nacho pushes Claudia through the doorway of the bus, and she steps down onto the desert floor. It's blazing hot, almost burning through her running shoes.

Nacho, as always, is big, fat, smiley, and cute. He pulls a bandana from his back pocket and blows his nose into it.

"Gross!" Claudia whispers.

Nacho smiles anyway. He folds the bandana over several times and uses it to wipe his brow. Claudia finds herself sweating too, and she can see the moisture oozing from the pores of her overweight companion. He's almost handsome; she has to admit. Perhaps after the long, upcoming trek, his fat will melt away, and he will be truly beautiful.

Tío Joaquín, Claudia's great uncle, one of her favorite people in the whole world, hobbles out of the bus next. He's an old man, in his late seventies, but eager to make his way into "the beautiful north," as he calls it. He points to a dip in the mountains that lay across the desolate valley.

"There," he says. "We must get to that point. It's only a seven-hour walk. The pass is low, and on the other side is the highway. There's a little shelter there. A bus will come by and pick us up within an hour. And then..." he smiles his old snaggle-toothed grin, "we'll be on our way to Florida."

"To start my flower shop," sighs Claudia.

"To pick oranges and enjoy the sweet life in America," adds Nacho, and his grin is even broader.

Seven other illegal immigrants step from the bus: Angela, a young woman; her son, Pepe, a boy of about twelve; and five strapping young men from the seaside town of Vera Cruz. They have each paid the border Coyotes one thousand pesos to be brought safely into the United States and then led across the searing floor of this terrible valley to the highway and a bus that will take them deep into the United States.

"Follow me," says Jesus Morales, the Coyote. He's a short man with a pencil-thin mustache, dangerous eyes, and an ugly scar across the side of his face. "We walk through the night and come to the highway at morning. Stay close; Look sharp. Stay together. If the border patrol finds you, I'll disappear. You'll never see me again, and you never heard of me either. Anyone who identifies me will die. I have associates who can be very cruel.

"Now stay together, move fast, and you, old man... remember your promise to keep up. If I find you falling behind, I cut you loose, and you're left here to die in the desert."

"If he falls," says Nacho, "I will carry him."

The Coyote smirks. "Carry yourself, Gordo. That's all I can expect of you."

"Don't worry, Uncle," says Claudia. "We will take care of you."

"Touching," says the Coyote. "Now, if you run out of water don't worry. We have a stash of water bottles along the way, and they'll keep you going."

The others nod. Claudia hoists her little backpack up onto her shoulder. She has only two bottles of water to get them through the seven-hour walk and is glad to hear of the Coyote's stash. She takes her uncle by the hand and falls in behind Morales.

Nacho carries a guitar. Claudia eyes it with a look of disgust. "You could buy a new one in Florida," she says.

"But we are lovers, this guitar and I."

"Let's see how you feel about her as we go up the mountains and your sweetheart has been on your back for hours," says the Coyote. "My bet is that you'll fall out of love quickly, and you'll leave her behind as soon as we begin to climb."

Nacho just shrugs and grins his notoriously silly smile. So many of the girls back in his hometown think he's dashing. He flips the guitar strap over his shoulder, slings the instrument behind him, and takes up a position beside Uncle Joaquín.

After a few more minutes of preparation, the walkers set out across the valley heading hopefully to freedom and prosperity.

#

Four hours into the trek and they are more than tired. Not one of them would have believed the desert heat. It is nearly one hundred degrees at two o'clock in the morning. They stumble through the dark night using their flashlights sparingly, relying on the limited brightness of the Crescent Moon. Claudia pulls out one of her little water bottles and raises it. There are only a few swallows left. She barely touches the water to her lips before she passes the bottle to her uncle.

"S' all right," he murmurs and pushes the bottle back to his niece. "Save it for yourself. I'm old. I need very little water."

Claudia hurries up to the Coyote. "And where is this supply of water you told us about, Mr. Morales?"

"Should be right up here," he tells her. And he shines his flashlight ahead and lets it search across the rock formations that cluster around them like watchful predators. "Well, maybe not yet."

"Perhaps you missed it, Señor," suggests Nacho as he moves up to them.

"I've been looking," says Morales. "Just haven't gotten to it... but we will. Trust me."

"Trust a Coyote?" Nacho laughs, and he reaches behind him and strums a dissident chord on his guitar. "You are the most untrustworthy of all God's creatures. Believe me, Mr. Morales. If I have learned anything from all the stories my mother told me when I was a little boy, it's that you can never trust a coyote."

"Well then you're shit out of luck aren't you?" says Morales and he moves ahead continuing to sweep the rock formations around them with his flashlight.


Another hour and the beam from Morales's flashlight illuminates a rock outcropping that resembles a coyote resting on its haunches.

"Ah, there you are, Hermano," he says to the rock formation. "We are two of a kind you and I. We are brothers."

At the base of the rocks, a large granite boulder with a crucifix painted on it looks like the headstone of a grave, perhaps a memorial to someone who died as they tried to navigate this desolate valley.

"Come, my friends," says Morales, "share," and several of the walkers rush ahead, dive under the outcropping and root around behind the boulder.

"It's no good," comes the cry of the first man to find the water bottles.

5

"Slit open!" the young woman calls.

"Empty," shouts another.

Morales rushes in. "Those bastards," he cries.

"Who would do this?" asks Claudia as she and Tío Joaquín make their way up to the others.

"La Migra?" asks Nacho.

"No," says Morales. "Not the damn border patrol. It's those fucking vigilantes. They don't want us in their country. They want to make sure we stay away. They'll do things La Migra would never do."

"What's the use," sighs Joaquín, and he sits down under the outcropping and buries his face in his hands.

"No," commands the Coyote. "We do not wait, we walk. Only another two hours to go. You can make it, old man. If we wait, the day will only get hotter."

"Come on, uncle," says Claudia and she pulls Joaquín to his feet.

"But I'm so hungry," whispers Angela.

"Me too," sighs Pepe, and he pitches his own empty water bottle down among the sliced up bottles under the tombstone.

"Move," says the Coyote and the walkers trudge on.


Another hour later, as dawn turns the sky to a soft shade of turquoise, the walkers struggle toward the summit of the mountain pass. Their knees burn with pain. Their faces are drawn. Nacho, who is not looking well himself, supports Tío Joaquín. Claudia struggles too. She now carries Nacho's guitar. Her empty bottles rattles against it as if trying to play some weird, unearthly music.

The sun now bursts above the mountain tops blasting its heat at them full force, making the walkers turn their eyes away... all except Claudia's uncle who faces the brightness as if to curse it. But instead, he cries out.

"Dios Mio! Can you see it? Can you see that?"

"What?" asks Nacho. He hasn't looked up from the ground for nearly an hour.

"Where?" Claudia wants to know.

"There, above the mountain pass," shouts Joaquín with whatever energy he has left.

They all look up, even the Coyote.

"Jesus!" he says.

"It's an optical illusion," one of the young men mumbles. "Like a mirage."

"Or a miracle," whispers Claudia.

They're looking at a shimmering blue triangle that floats high in the air above them. Water seems to fill it.

"What does it want with us?" asks Angela.

"To give us a drink," says Nacho as his grin grows hopefully.

"We're hallucinating, that's all," says the Coyote. "I've never heard of anything like this before."

"Stay away from it," growls Joaquín. "It may be an alien spacecraft ready to send out lightning bolts to kill us all."

"Or rain on us," says Nacho, and just as he does, there's a downpour. Water cascades onto him as though the triangle was his own personal spring shower. And there's a crack of thunder.

"Ka-BLAM!" shouts Nacho in response. "It's so cool, and so damn wet!"

The others follow, each bolting under the watery triangle. Claudia rushes to open her water bottles and hold them up so that they can catch as much water as possible. Angela helps her.

Pepe dances in the puddles that form on the parched earth. Tío Joaquín stretches out his arms and lets the wetness wash over him. The boys from Vera Cruz wrestle in the rain. They rub their hands in each other's hair, take off their shirts and bathe half naked in the downpour. Their shirts get drenched, turn into washcloths that will keep them cool for the time until they reach the highway.

"A miracle, that's all," says Angela. "Like Moses in the desert. God sent us water."

"Why didn't he ever do it before?" asks Morales. "So many have died out here. What makes us so special?"

As if in response, new thunder rumbles across the sky. It's the roar of a jet that cuts in front of the sun, throwing them all into momentary darkness like the effect of some sudden eclipse. And with that, the triangle winks out of existence.

The walkers look at each other in sadness and confusion.

"I had hoped it would accompany us all the way to the highway," murmurs Angela.

Claudia says, "But it did save us. Our water bottles are full."

"I feel a thousand percent stronger," says Nacho. "Come on Joaquín, let's go."

This way," says Morales, and he moves to the front of the group and leads them on toward the summit.

#

Looking down on the very cleft in the mountains that the walkers are trying to reach two men study the vacant desert.

"Not much going on tonight," says Clayton Bailey. "Guess I'll head back to the ranch."

He's a tall man with broad shoulders and muscular arms. Still, his face seems innocent, arrogant, lost... but angry as dirt. He wears a baby blue cowboy hat, shirt, jeans, and boots. He stands beside his massive silver Ram pickup sipping a Lone Star Beer, and talking with his pal, Andy Myers.

"Yep, we might as well cash it in," says Andy. He tries to spit a wad of tobacco juice, but it dribbles over his scraggly beard and onto his faded cowboy shirt.

"But what the..."

There's sudden motion at the distant mountain pass. It catches his attention, and he raises his binoculars to take a look.

"Well I'll be dipped in cow shit," says Meyers. "Good thing we didn't give up. They made it through."

"More visitors from the south?" asks Bailey.

"Yep, right through Devil's Canyon."

"More freeloaders and bloodsuckers marching in here like they own the God damn place."

"Ya got that right, Lone Stranger."

Baily reaches over to the back of his pickup, sets down the beer and grabs his six-shooter. Casually, he aims into the pass, then pulls the gun back and begins carefully loading bullets that sparkle like silver.

"Did I ever tell ya how I got the name Lone Stranger?" he asks.

"Only a million times. But I like the story. Why not tell it again while our visitors come out into the open."

"Okay," says Bailey. "You know I hate Mex-kins, right?"

"Almost as much as I do."

"They're basically a dirty people, Andy. Mud people I like ta call 'em – dark skinned, foul smelling. They're not too bright either, and they sure as hell can't fight.

"I once captured some seventy-six of 'em at the same time. That was during the American Civil War."

"The War Between the States, eh," adds a scruffy redheaded seventeen year old who climbs out the pickup and takes a seat across from Bailey.

"Hey, Toronto," says Bailey.

"Hi, Uncle Stranger," says the kid as he settles in.

"It was in the wake of the battle of Bull Run," Bailey continues. "Right here in the great state of Texas. All these Mex-kins was pouring in across the border. I was here with General Ulysses S. Grant... top general of the Confederate States of America."

Meyers nods enthusiastically. Toronto flinches, looks questioningly at his uncle.

'Don't need that look, boy," Bailey tells the kid. "I was there, also at the Battle of the Bulge, Battle of New Orleans, Saratoga, Agincourt, Thermopylae, the siege of Troy. I've lived a hundred lives as a warrior, and seen a thousand battles."

Toronto just nods.

"So Grant turns to me and says, 'Son, I'm afraid I'm going to have to ask you to risk your life for the South."

"And I say, 'General Grant, it would be an honor.'

"'Okay then, get out there and scout around a bit,' he says. 'See what you can find. But if you get caught, yer on your own, understand?'

"I do, but still I ride up over the ridge. And there they are, those Mex-kin mud people having a powwow with the Indians, making their liberal pinko plans to set up a welfare state right here in the south.

"And I just lose it, you know. I take the reigns to my horse, put 'em in my mouth, bite down, grab a sawed-off shotgun in each hand, and charge 'em. I kill about five hundred the first time through. Another hundred and fifty of 'em run back across the border. As I say, they're a cowardly people.

"Course I get pretty well shot up myself. My baby blue confederate uniform's ripped to shreds by tommy hawks an machetes. Still, I'm able to corral the rest of them ignorant pinkos. I line 'em up and drive 'em back to the army post. And you know, they're so damn cowardly that they surrender to General Grant right then and there."

Toronto looks perplexed but doesn't interrupt.

"Unfortunately," continues Bailey, "I'm shot up so bad that the old general doesn't even recognize me. He says, 'did you just capture all these cowardly indigenous peoples alone, Stranger?'"

And of course, I say, "sure thing General Grant, for the good a the South."

"And that's how the legend of the Lone Stranger got born," says Andy.

"That's not the civil war I learned about in school," says Toronto.

"Didn't you go to school in Canada?" asks Bailey.

"Well sure, but we studied the history of all North America."

Are you questioning me, boy?" growls Bailey. "Remember I was THERE."

"General Grant led the North not the South, and it was over a hundred and fifty years ago," says the kid.

"Did you ever stop to think that those Canadian pinkos who write those school books of yours jumbled up the facts just to make the south look bad?"

"No sir."

"Well, they just might have. Next thing you know they'll be wanting to tear down statues a Jefferson Davis and Stonewall Jackson all over Dixie."

Toronto lowers his eyes in total disillusionment. Bailey recognizes the look, walks over, and ruffles the boy's hair.

"Hey," he says with an innocent grin, "You know even eye-witnesses have the right to embellish a little, don't ya, add a few extra facts here an there."

"So that what you're doing, eh?"

"Damn straight, son... embellishin' ta make sure everyone understands my point. It's the point that matters after all not the facts."

"Yes, sir. I guess I understand," But Toronto's smile quickly fades, and again he looks troubled.

#

11

The walkers have almost made it down the hill. But the sight of the Lone Stranger and his monster truck silhouetted against the big American sky screams at them like a warning. And then they see the tall man in baby blue lower his pistol and take a shot in their direction. Jesus Morales feels the bullet rip into his arm.

"Jesus!" says Jesus, as his blood splatters everyone around him.

The others scatter. Tío Joaquín , who had been a model of strength through the last hour of the walk, is suddenly unable to keep up. He falls behind the others until he and Claudia are nearly alone.

Two of the men race toward the highway and the little shelter beside it. Pepe and Angela turn and run back toward the mountains. Claudia and her uncle follow Nacho and the others as they turn west toward an arroyo where twisted trees offer a place to hide.

Bailey pushes up his hat with the nose of his pistol and casually fires another shot!

Uncle Joaquín falls with an ear-splitting cry.

"Balacianron mis nalgas!" he screams. "THEY SHOT ME IN THE ASS!"

Claudia turned to him in disbelief.

"My ass feels like it's gone, Mija," he croaks, "Maybe my hip too."

Joaquín's backside is a bloody mess. Claudia reaches into her pack, pulls out a bottle of water and moves it toward her uncle's lips, but he smashes it out of her hand.

"Not water, TEQUILA!" he shouts deliriously and then grimaces and begins to moan, "My poor dumb ass!"

Nacho backtracks toward Claudia and Joaquín.

"Go on, Nacho," the young woman calls.

The fat man moves closer. Unknowingly, he has stepped right into the sites of Andy Meyers high-powered rifle.

Claudia sees the gunmen on the rise. "Get out of here, Nacho, before someone shoots you."

Nacho turns with a jerky motion, trips over his own feet, stumbles and falls. It saves his life. A bullet whizzes over his head just as the thwap, thwap of helicopter blades slice the morning air.

Nacho gets to his feet and hobbles off toward the ravine.

"Stay where you are!" a loudspeaker calls from the chopper. But just then another series of shots whiz by the walkers. The shots seem to distract the chopper crew, and Nacho is able to dive into the brush beside the wash.

Now two INS vehicles plow into the area. Six border patrol agents (La Migra) jump from the trucks and begin rounding up the walkers. It's fairly easy. The Americans are armed, and the immigrants stop running as soon as the vehicles arrive.

#

Up on the bluff, The Lone Stranger takes another gulp of beer and belches long and low.

"Good one," says Meyers as he gives the big guy a fist bump and then raises his binoculars to study the walkers.

"Mmmmm, Mamacita," he calls as he spots Claudia. "Coochie, coochie. You can escape inta my bed any time day or night."

"Personally, I wouldn't touch her greasy ass with a ten-foot pole," Baily growls.

"I think she could keep me plenty warm on our cold Texas nights," says Andy. "Here, take a closer look." And he passes his binoculars to the big guy.

Bailey raises them to his eyes and studies Claudia as she's being led into the custody of the INS.

"Soft, kissable lips," he says with a smile. "Dark, lustrous hair that swirls about her face like that veil of some mysterious princess."

"Really?"

"The starry eyes of a dreamer that nevertheless hold the promise of strength and leadership."

"Who you lookin at?" asks Myers.

"Large, firm, lovely breasts!"

"Yeah, that's her."

Toronto has his own set of binoculars, and he's also watching the action. "Too bad, eh, Mr. Myers," he says. "You know, they'll just take her back across the border and drop her on the other side."

"What a waste," says Meyers. "I'd just love to warm my feet on that sweet Senorita's bottom every night."

"Warm your clodhoppers on a wetback?" Bailey laughs as he moves toward the front of his truck, "Sounds like you're lookin' for a bad case a Montezuma's Foot, amigo. Ouch!"

Myers chuckles.

"Better get outta here, eh," says Toronto.

"And why would we do that?"

"Well, you bloodied a couple of them pretty badly, and they fell damn hard."

"Just doin my part for the great state of Texas," says Bailey. "And besides, no one got hurt. They're not real people, you know... just Mex' kins."

"Only...." says Toronto.

"Only what?" growls Bailey.

"Nothin'," says the kid as he and Bailey hop back into the truck. The Lone Stranger let's out a "Yippee-ai-oh," slams his ride into gear, and peels out. As he does, he hits his horn, which sounds the first few notes of The Yellow Rose of Texas.

"I'm back in the saddle again, you mother lovin cy-utes!" he calls as they ride off.

# Chapter Two

As the morning sun sears into the Texas desert, a Jeep Wrangler roars over the open terrain near the interstate. It spins out, does a donut, then another. Its top is down, and it's blowing dust everywhere. But that doesn't seem to bother the driver at all.

She's short, blond, cute, wearing a cowboy hat that would blow away if she didn't reach up frequently and press it down hard onto her head.

"Yee hah!" she screams, does another donut, suddenly spins too close to the edge of a gully, and both wheels on the passenger side sink into it.

"Fuck," says the cowgirl as she pushes the door open and climbs out. She's wearing a light denim pair of daisy duke shorts and pink cowgirl boots. Her white cotton blouse is tied in a knot under her breasts, exposing a slim, well-tanned waistline.

"What am I supposed to do now, you stupid piece of shit?" she shouts at the jeep, and she kicks the rear tire that's buried halfway in the dust.

She looks up at the sky, shakes her head, and begins to walk all the way around the vehicle again. "In another hour it'll be hot enough to melt the tires... and me."

She scrambles up to the car door, pulls it open, and reaches inside to get her cell phone. Tipping her cowgirl hat down over her eyes to blot out the blazing sun, she studies the phone, dials a number, and then curses again. "No fucking reception."

She types a text message and hits "send." There's no sound; the message goes nowhere. "Like, HELLO," she sighs and walks over to a large boulder across from the jeep and sits down.

Suddenly Nacho struggles up from the ravine. He's sweatier than ever and covered with dust. He works his way past the Jeep, takes out his bandanna, still wet from the miraculous rain, wipes his face, sees the cowgirl, and takes a big step backward.

"Oh hi, cowboy," she says showing no fear of the stranger. "I like your guitar."

Nacho smiles back and then takes in the scene. "Hey, maybe I can help you Miss," he says. "You and your Jeep look like you need a hand."

"My jeep sure does," she answers with a welcoming smile. "And you do look strong enough. If you leaned into it, I'll bet we could get her out of here."

"Absolutely," Nacho answers, and he runs several paces into the open country, pulls his guitar off of his shoulder, and begins to set it down in the brush.

"Oh no," says the young woman. "Let me take it, put it in the Jeep. Once we get going again, I'll give you a ride into town."

"Nice," says Nacho.

"Britney."

"Britney?"

"Like, my name is Britney... and you are?"

Nacho thinks for a moment and bows.

"Francisco Alfredo Gonzales Gonzales Gonzales."

"So, Gonzales three times?"

"But you can call me Nacho."

16

"Cute name... you're cute too," says Britney. "So, let's rescue my jeep right now, before it gets any hotter?"

"Si Señorita," says Nacho with that big crazy grin.

Nacho is strong, and Britney must be an old hand at driving her Jeep out of off-road gullies, because after only two tries, the wheels spin, Nacho leans hard against the bumper, lifts it as he does, and the Wrangler rises out of the dust and pulls out onto the hardpan.

"Yee hah," the cowgirl cheers. "Get in here cowboy, and I'll take you wherever you want to go."

"Someplace that has a nice warm shower, and I can change into some clean clothes."

"Sounds like my apartment," says Britney.

"All right then."

Nacho reaches into the back seat of the Jeep, grabs his guitar, and begins strumming and singing as Britney steers the vehicle up onto the interstate and heads back toward town.

#

"Ay, ay, ay, ay," Nacho sings in the shower. He hasn't felt this clean in weeks. Not with the kind of hard soap that Britney gave him. "Kinda macho," he thinks. "Wonder where she got it? Does she run a home for wayward cowboys?"

He laughs. If so, he's in luck.

He looks around the little bathroom with the pink wallpaper, shelves neatly arranged with rows of shampoos, soaps, shaving cream, there's even a man's razor, right next to the statue of a little pink pony. Is she married? He wonders. No ring.

In the living room, the cowgirl has laid out a whole new set of clothing for him. She'll gather up his dust-caked duds later, wash them, mend them, and give them back to him. In the meantime, the leftover shirts and jeans and underwear from her last serious cowboy will more than do the job. Lucky for Nacho, he was a big dude and a little overweight. Lucky too that he's now living somewhere in Montana. He won't be around to accuse Nacho of wearing his clothes or stealing his girl. Except that there are other men still interested in Britney, one in particular and Nacho is lucky that he doesn't end up dressed in baby blue.

Britney's apartment is spotless and uncluttered. The living room has white wallpaper with little bows on it. The big television sits on a white cabinet whose shelves are piled high with music videos by country and western singers. A picture above her tan corduroy couch shows Shania Twain in concert. The words scrawled below the sexy songstress proclaim, "Man, I feel like a woman."

Britney's white queen sized bed almost fills her tiny bedroom. The matching dresser at the foot of the bed features a few pictures: her parents, herself as a five-year-old girl with her first rifle, and the ominous image of Clayton Bailey. Above all of this is a mirror with more than a few blue ribbons hanging from the corners of the frame. They're awards for sharp shooting. It appears that Nacho's savior is more than a good housekeeper; she's a crack shot.

Nacho keeps scrubbing and singing.

Britney tunes his guitar. She listens for a moment, picks out his key and begins to accompany him. Then she starts singing along.

Inside the shower, he stops and listens. He can't believe his ears; the voice from the other room must belong to an angel, he thinks. Maybe Claudia's sister is right: America is heaven.

A few moments later (after a mild argument over whether or not Nacho will wear the clothes Britney has given him) they sit at the kitchen table. Nacho looks good in the new outfit. He drinks a coke and tries to explain why he crossed the border.

"All we want to do is work," he says, "the people from my village. But there are no jobs. There was such a celebration when they opened the auto plant in our state. Five years later it's closed, and all the work has gone to China.

"I was on the assembly line myself, inspecting door handles. It's a critical job, you know. If your door handles don't work, you can't get into your car."

Britney giggles. This cowboy really is fun. "So, you decided to come across."

"My friend Claudia has a sister who crossed over legally. She works in the fields harvesting melons. She says such wonderful things about your country and the man she works for...."

"She works around here?"

"Somewhere nearby, yes. She picks melons. Anyway, I just wanted to come over. Claudia wants to travel to Florida and open a flower shop. I don't care. Flowers or melons, it's all the same to me. I think picking melons is just as important as inspecting door handles don't you?"

"Of course," says Britney as she begins to twist her fingers into her long blonde hair.

"But that is no longer possible, is it?"

"Inspecting door handle's or growing melons?"

"Crossing over."

"Yes. They've closed the border and are making it impossible for honest workers to come here and get jobs."

Britney shrugs. "I think politics sucks."

"Well, okay but you know, the only way to enter the country legally now is to enter it illegally! There's no more legal way in, so illegal has become the only legal way."

Britney shakes her head in confusion. "Whatever."

19

"It didn't work for us anyway. La Migra intercepted us and shot Claudia's poor old uncle. Then they carted everyone back to Sonora. And now I'm here alone, trying to find a place that will help me stay safe. Maybe Florida."

"Maybe Eden," says Britney.

"I don't think so," Nacho answers. "I read the bible. That place has a tougher border than this one. And I hear their snakes are worse than rattlers."

Britney laughs out loud. "I meant Eden Melon Ranch," she says. "It's just west of here. The boy who owns it is a real sweetheart. His name is Nick Fleming."

"A boy owns a ranch."

Britney giggles and suddenly runs her hand over Nacho's shoulder.

"No, silly; he's a grown man, I just call him a boy the way I call any guy I like a boy... like you... boy."

"I'm a boy too?"

"Like a hottie, I think." And she kisses Nacho on the lips and then jumps to her feet.

"Come on."

"Where?"

"To visit the boy who owns Eden Melon Ranch. He happens to be my brother."

Nacho shakes his head in confusion.

Britney walks back to him, gives him another quick kiss, takes him by the arm and leads him out into the Texas heat.

# Chapter Three

Padre Carlos is in his late fifties, a saintly looking man in spite of the expression of annoyance that now darkens his face. Loud sobs fill his church, and he grimaces as they become even louder when he turns from the altar during his morning mass and makes his way to the pulpit.

"Ooooh, Blessed Maria. Nooo!" A large woman with gray hair, circles under her eyes, and a jowly face sobs into her bright red handkerchief.

"Ohhh Noooo!"

Padre Carlos grimaces again as he takes his place at the top of the pulpit.

"Beloved congregation...." he begins.

"Ohhh nooo!"

"And you too, Lucinda."

"We have gathered this morning to pray that God will restore the health and well-being of our beloved brother, Joaquín."

He eyes Claudia who sits between blubbering Aunt Lucinda and a man who looks very much like her Uncle Joaquín. It's his brother, Rafael. She's doing her best to comfort her aunt and contain her own sadness.

"We were put on this earth my brothers and sisters," the priest continues, "to serve the Lord, but also to provide for the

21

well being and safety of our loved ones." He looks over the crowd. The church is full this Sunday morning, as it is every Sunday and Holy Day.

"Providing for our loved ones," he continues, "requires sacrifice."

"Ohhh nooo!"

"Yes, Lucinda. Sometimes we are called upon to deny ourselves and be humble so that we have the ability to give. But at other times," and here the priest turns his eyes to Claudia, "we must stand tall in the face of oppression. We must be brave."

"We must make a statement. We must let those who have wronged us know that we will no longer suffer in silence. We must not allow our children and loved ones to pay the price for our cowardice."

"Ohhh nooo!"

"Oh yes, Lucinda. A bullet from the rifle of a U. S. border patrolman wounded your brother-in-law. And now it is time for us to help the Americans understand that we will no longer suffer this persecution. We will stand up to them. We will make a statement."

"We can do it!" The priest shouts in the war cry of the Mexican Revolution, "Si Se Puede!" And now he finds himself staring directly at Claudia who seems frightened by what the priest is saying.

"Can we?" she murmurs to her aunt and shakes her head.

"Ohhh nooo!" moans Tía Lucinda.

"Si Se Puede!" shouts uncle Rafael.

"Now go forth," the priest insists. "Be brave my brothers and sisters and seek justice.

"Si Se Puede!" he shouts.

But in the very back of the church, a young man named Antonio shakes his head, lowers his eyes in disillusionment, and leaves.

# Chapter Four

Listen, Vieja floja," Julio says. "You pick cantaloupe this way!" And he bends down and, carefully pressing his long fingers against the base of the fruit; he pops the melon off the vine. "It's so damn easy!"

Julio stands tall and sticks out his chest. He is a handsome man (he thinks) in a slim, wiry kind of way. Julio looks down at Maria who is still bending over the plant, still wrestling with the vine and the base of the next fruit. He falls to his knees beside her, reaches over, and pops off another melon.

"Do I have to come here every day and show you how to do it right?"

"Of course not, sir. I'm very sorry," Maria says. "I thought I was doing it correctly."

Julio loves being next to the girl. She is so young and so beautiful: dark eyes, long black hair, full lips and lovely dimples when she smiles. Even dimples when she frowns, which she is doing now and always seems to do whenever Julio comes by. The whole relationship makes him angry.

"If you were doing it correctly, would I be standing here talking to you, wasting my time, wasting the boss's money, wasting the opportunity for some other, better worker to come and enjoy our warm sunny fields and exceptional working conditions?"

Maria sighs. "No sir."

She is doing her best not to cry (or to show her anger--she would like to kick Julio right in the cajones and tromp on him with the new boots her sister has sent her from Mexico).

"I'll try harder, next time," she says instead.

"See that you do," answers Julio as he walks away.

Maria bends down and does her best to "pop" the cantaloupe off the next vine.

"He loves you, you know," someone whispers. It's Maria's friend Lola. "He only does that so he can be close to you."

"He will never get close to me, Mija," Maria answers. "Every time he comes near me I feel myself growing faint... and not in a nice way, in a sick way."

"I think he's cute."

"Good, then the next time he comes by to instruct me on the proper way to pick melons, I will refer him to you... and you can listen to the lesson and that strange 'sweet talk' of his."

"Julio," the women suddenly hear someone calling to the foreman in a decidedly American voice.

"Yeah, boss," Julio answers.

Maria looks up across the rows and sees Nick Fleming, owner of the ranch, calling to Julio.

"Now there's a real man," Maria sighs.

"Gringo!" curses Lola. "You can have him... but you'll never get him, of course."

"Of course," answers Maria. "I'm sure he has his plenty of Americana girls who flirt with him all the time. What would he want with someone like me?"

"Oh, Mujer, I wish I had your looks," says Lola. "You're beautiful, Maria. But also... you're right."

"Although..." Maria finds herself admitting with just a touch of hope in her voice, "Señor Fleming is angry with the foreman."

"It has nothing to do with us, I'm sure."

"Then why is he gesturing our way? Can you hear what he's saying?"

Lola squints as though closing her eyes will improve her hearing.

She is amazed at what Mr. Nick is saying and doesn't know if she should repeat it. Apparently, the gringo boss was calling Julio out for speaking so harshly to 'those lovely Mexican girls.'

Yes, realizes Lola, he had referred to both of them as 'lovely.'

Nick says, "Work is hard enough for them."

"Sí, Señior," the foreman answers.

"Their productivity is very high whether they are picking the melons your way or not."

"Sí, Señior."

"I'll have a word with them, myself," Nick adds. But before he can even move toward Lola and Maria, Britney's Jeep plows into the field and screeches to a stop right in front of him.

"Hey there, bro," she calls as she jumps down from the driver's seat, runs up to him, and gives him a hug.

"Hey there yourself," Nick answers as he smiles at Britney. "Didn't expect to see you today."

"Got a recruit for you."

The singing cowgirl motions for Nacho to get down from the other side of the Jeep, and he does slowly, but with a big smile on his face.

"This handsome hombre helped me dig my car out of a ditch over by the border wall," she says.

"Hola, Señor," beams Nacho.

Nick nods. "Crossed illegally?"

Nacho doesn't answer, doesn't nod, but doesn't lose that charming smile either. "It was a very hot morning," he says. "I saw that this pretty young woman was in trouble and felt that she needed my help."

"Like, I'd have been stuck out there in the broiling sun all afternoon if it hadn't been for this handsome dude."

Nacho's smile broadens, and he points to himself proudly. "Handsome Dude!"

"Know how to pick melons?" Nick asks.

"Señior, there is no melon that I cannot pick."


As they watch the trio talking only a few yards from them, Maria suddenly lets out a squeal and begins running down the row of melons toward them. She finally jumps up into Nacho's arms.

"Nacho, mi dulce, mi flor," she shouts as she gives him several big kisses.

"Mi pequeña hermana," says Nacho, and he holds her out at arm's length to study her.

"Actually, she is not my little sister," Nacho says to Nick, "but we have been friends since we were children back in our little village."

"I see," says Britney with perhaps a touch of concern in her voice.

"Excuse me, Señior... Miss...." Maria says to the Americans, "Sorry to interrupt, but it is such a treat to see Nacho after so many years."

"I'm sure it is," says Britney. Then she turns to Nick.

"So, what will it be, bro?"

"She *is* your little sister?" Nacho asks Nick.

"My real little sister... yes she is."

"Then I am in luck. I must already be employed. After all, who can say no to his little sister?"

"How well do you know my lil sis?" asks Nick.

"After I rescued her Jeep, she let me use her shower, she gave me new clothes to wear. That's all, no more than that."

Nick smiles. "Well, you're lucky. If she had gotten her hooks into you, you would be indebted to her for life."

"That's all, Señor? Just for life?"

"For starters," Nick answers with a laugh. "After that...."

"Then perhaps, Señior, you would be good enough to give me a job and save me from her."

"And you say you can pick melons?"

"Pop them right off the vine with my thumbs, yes I can do that."

"Okay, you're hired. Minimum wage. Hours – 7 AM to 7 PM. Half an hour for lunch. You sleep in the bunkhouse.

"See that ugly Mexican over there?"

"The one with the handsome mustache, the good looking, wiry guy?"

"If you say so," Nick says. "He's the foreman. I'll bring him around a little later and introduce you to him. He'll be happy to get an added hand. In the meantime, Maria, take him over to the living quarters and get him all set up."

"Yes, sir."

"And thank you, sir," says Nacho with that irrepressible smile. "And thank you too, Miss Britney."

"Hey," answers the girl, "Aren't you going to kiss me good bye."

"Will you then have your hooks into me then, Señorita?"

"It'll be a good start."

"Nacho, I don't think..." Maria begins, but he is already moving toward Britney, already has his arms around her, is already kissing her seriously.

"Whoa, cowboy," says Britney as she staggers back from the charming Mexican.

"Feel free to bring your hooks around me anytime, Miss," Nacho tells her. But Britney is looking at Maria whose eyes blaze accusingly.

"What?" the cowgirl asks.

"We all love Nacho," Maria says. "Please don't hurt him."

"Nick, have I ever hurt anyone?" the cowgirl asks.

The owner of the ranch raises his hands in surrender and takes a big step backward. "Leave me out of this, Ladies," he says. Then he steps forward again, shakes Nacho's hand, turns, and heads off to find Julio and explain whatever he can about their new employee.

# Chapter Five

Tragic, old Tía Lucinda sits at a table in the back of the Faithful Chicken Bar in Chubasco, Sonora, Mexico. She's sobbing as usual.

"Dios Mío," she moans for maybe the hundredth time, "My poor brother-in-law, once such a handsome gentleman, and now those damn Americans have robbed him of his manhood."

"At his age what does he care about his manhood anyway," grumbles her husband, Tío Rafael.

"To hell with his pecker. Those gringos shot his ass off. An old man without a prick is just another old man. But without his ass he is nothing. He can't sit down; he can't lie down, he can't even take a proper shit!"

Rafael sits beside Lucinda nursing a sweaty bottle of beer. Across from the couple, Padre Carlos stares into his glass of tequila and speaks without even looking up.

"Let's be honest, amigos," he says. "It's emblematic of the way our friendly neighbors to the north feel about our people. They don't love us."

"No," moans Lucinda. "They don't even like us."

"They fucking hate us," says Rafael.

Lucinda suddenly straightens up, turns to her husband and slams him with her purse.

"Watch your language, stupido. There are ladies present."

Across the room, Claudia sits with the young man who stood in the back of the church.

"So you're new in town then, Mr. Cervantes," she says.

He nods. "Moved up from Tampico."

"And have you read the great author who shares your name?"

"I'm not much of a reader."

"How can you not have read the greatest novel ever written?"

"Don Quixote?" he asks. "Doesn't interest me. It's just a story about a dreamer."

"I love dreamers," says Claudia. "When I was a little girl, Tía Lucinda used to tell me that I was the greatest dreamer in our village."

He smiles. "I'm not sure that's a compliment."

"So then, Antonio," she continues. "If you're not a dreamer what are you?"

"I'm a realist. Take that little speech the padre made in church. It was dreams... nothing but raw dreams. Do you really think anyone here can have an impact on that monstrosity up north?"

"Of course."

"Dreamer! The north has all the money, all the military, and all the jobs. I say let them make themselves crazy with their ambition and paranoia. Let them get fat and stupid and lazy. Let them blow themselves up. As long as they leave us alone."

Claudia leans away from the man and shakes her head.

"Why am I even here with you?"

He smiles. "I invited you to dinner. I knew that you were a dreamer, but that fire in your eyes is so exciting that I thought I could put up with your illusions."

"And can you, Señor?"

"Not if you agree with Padre Carlos that people in a tiny border town can have any effect on the policies of two enormous nations."

"Well I DO believe it, and if you don't, then you don't have to be part of any of this."

"Of what?"

Suddenly a new voice intrudes.

"Of the glorious revenge this beautiful lady dreams of, my friend."

Claudia and Antonio turn and see a small man with a handsome mustache, expensive shoes and a well-tailored, silk suit walking toward their table. He's carrying a bottle of Tequila and three shot glasses.

"Thank you," Claudia tells the man.

"My name is Emilio," he says. His eyes are dark. His smile is frightening.

"May I join you?"

Claudia looks at him warily.

"Be my guest," says the young man.

Emilio takes a seat across from Antonio, beside Claudia, and begins pouring three glasses of tequila.

"None for me," says Claudia.

But the well-dressed man pours anyway. He slides a glass over to Antonio and takes a long slow sip himself.

"Let me tell you, Señor and Señorita," he begins. "You *can* get even with those American cabrones," he pauses and smiles, "if you are willing to do to them what they do to each other in their country."

"And what is that?"

Emilio leans forward and leers at Antonio, then he turns to Claudia. "You know what I mean, don't you, young lady?"

"It sounds to me like you and Antonio are two of a kind," answers Claudia. She rolls her eyes, takes the glass of tequila, and downs it in one shot.

31

"If you want the folks up north to take you seriously, you have to hurt them," says Emilio.

"Hurt is not what I'm after, says Claudia, "nor is revenge."

"What then?"

Claudia sighs. "I'm not exactly sure... I have to think more about it: maybe understanding... respect... something like that."

"You *are* a dreamer princess," says Emilio, "the worst kind: a dreamer who doesn't even understand her own dreams."

He laughs then gestures for the young couple to lean in closer to him. "Let me tell you my friends, there are weaknesses in El Norte. There are holes in their defenses and their philosophy. These are things that a strong couple like yourselves could take advantage of."

"Do you have any specifics, amigo," asks Antonio. Claudia looks from one man to the other and starts to think that their expressions are tragically similar.

"FUCK EM," says Emilio as he turns to Claudia. "You understand that don't you, pretty lady. A girl like you could bring them to their knees. Couldn't she, Antonio?"

The younger man just shrugs.

"If there's one thing those gringos understand," Emilio continues, "it's a good screwing. They've been doing it to our people for years, and they'll keep on doing it until we make it so uncomfortable for them that they decide that they've had enough, and they'll simply have to go and screw someone else."

Emilio takes another sip from his glass and pours more tequila all around. He tries to move closer to Claudia, but she pulls away. And that's when a large firm hand falls on Emilio's shoulder.

It's Padre Carlos.

"Ah Padre. Has the church censured you yet... asked you to put an end to your rabble rousing sermons?"

The Padre ignores his comment and tightens his grip on the man's shoulder.

"What are you doing here, Emilio?" he asks.

The small man smiles coldly. "I was only making polite conversation."

"Well, don't."

"They're drinking my tequila, aren't they?"

The Padre sighs. "So then, how is your brother?"

Emilio grimaces as though he doesn't really want to talk about his brother. Finally he just sighs.

"Doing well, of course."

"And his business?"

"Thriving."

"And your relationship?"

Emilio smiles his crafty smile. "Good as always. We're partners, you know."

"Indeed," says the priest. "I guess that means he's talking to you again."

"Let's just say he understands the good I can bring to his empire. Like introducing him to Claudia here."

The priest's grip on Emilio's shoulder tightens even more. "Don't you think Claudia's suffered enough? She talked her uncle into going across the border with her and now he lies in bed, a shadow of the man he was only a week ago."

"In my opinion, he was never much of a man," says Emilio.

That last remark seems so disrespectful that Claudia turns to him in anger.

"Señior, I don't know who you think you are, but *both* of my uncles rode with Pancho Villa. They are heroes."

Emilio takes a quick look over at Tío Rafael who is still arguing with his blustery wife. "Well, that would make your uncles about one hundred and fifty years old," he says. "The way that one is acting maybe he is. But do you think he's still man enough to help you get even with those bastards up north?"

"I told you," Claudia answers. "This isn't about revenge, or guilt, it's about...." She looks down at her hands, bites her lip, stars for a moment at Antonio in disappointment, then she gets to her feet, pushes her way past the priest, and rushes out into the night.

# Chapter Six

Nick Fleming deftly sidesteps the soccer ball as it comes spinning across the dry hardpan in front of the row of simple but well-kept little buildings. His company provides them as housing for the migrant workers. He turns to see Maria's little son, Juanito, move quickly behind the ball, and then the kid powers a kick that sends the ball flying toward Nacho. The big man steps back, jumps at just the right moment, and heads the ball back to the kid.

"Ka-BLAM!" says Nacho as his head strikes the ball and sends it flying. But Juanito is right there to stop the ball with his chest. He sees it drop to his feet, and begins dribbling toward his mother's friend.

Nick makes it up onto the porch of Maria's little home just in time to turn and see the kid feint one way, send Nacho sprawling the other, and then drive the ball between two pink cones that the workers have set out as a soccer goal.

"YES!" calls the boy as he raises his arms in triumph and runs around the lot whooping and cheering.

Nick smiles and steps inside the little building.

Maria is washing dishes in a small sink at the back of the room. She turns and looks with surprise at the owner of Eden Melon Ranch.

"Hola," says Nick with a smile.

"Mr. Nick," the woman answers, "to what do I owe this honor."

Nick feels strangely nervous. After all, he's calling on an employee. Still, he realizes that, even with strands of hair untucked from the band she wears on her head, even without any makeup (or maybe because of it) she's beautiful.

Maria recognizes his nervousness the way any woman recognizes the actions of a man who finds her attractive. She takes a deep breath and turns to face him.

"Is there something I can do for you, Sir?"

Nick fidgets. Maria thinks it's cute for a tall, well-built man to be nervous in her presence. Even though she only wears jeans and a simple blue cotton blouse, it makes her feel very attractive.

"I just wanted to remind you," Nick begins, still looking uncertain, "that the crew will be spraying the fields tomorrow, and you need to wear gloves. The chemicals can get on your hands. They can be a little dangerous."

"Are you going around telling this to all the workers?" Maria asks with a smirk.

Nick suddenly smiles, seems surer of himself. "I was hoping that you and a few of the other leaders would pass the message on."

Maria likes the fact that he calls her a leader. But she's equally sure that this was hardly the reason he stopped. She knows that there are many young women among the workers who would gladly make their way up to his big house and spend all evening... all night in fact. But here he is, talking to her, a mother with a little boy.

"I'll gladly pass the message on, Mr. Nick," she says giving him her warmest smile.

"Great," answers Nick and turns to go. But just as he reached for the door, Maria quickly adds, "Can I make you some coffee?"

Nick stops, turns, and nods.

A few minutes later, as he and Maria sit at her little kitchen table looking out as Nacho and her son play soccer... sometimes cheering like little kids, occasionally almost looking like athletes, Nick nods toward Nacho and asks, "So, he's the father?"

"What?"

Maria can't believe it. Is this the reason that the boss has come all the way out to her little shack, to ask about Nacho?

"I'm sorry... is that too personal a question?" Nick asks.

Maria smiles. "It's the kind of question any boss might ask about a new employee, I guess."

"It might be illegal to ask a question like that."

"Really?"

Maria shakes her head. "This is a crazy country where a boss can't even ask about a woman and her relationship with another worker."

"Workers rights."

"I'm an illegal immigrant, Sir; I have no rights."

Nick smiles. "On my farm you do."

Maria takes a sip of coffee. She thinks she would do anything to keep this handsome man sitting here just a little longer. She loves the way he looks at her, not in any lustful way either. She's had plenty of those looks. Nick's stare is so interested, so attentive.

"Do you have a moment," she asks.

Nick nods as though he too wants nothing more than to sit with her all afternoon.

"Okay, then," she says. "Let me tell you about Juanito's father."

#

37

"When we were little girls," she begins, "everyone in the village thought that my sister, Claudia, and I were wonderful. Mama taught us how to sing Mexican Ranchera Songs and, when we were only five and six, we started to perform every Friday night from the back of our Uncle Joaquín's old, flatbed truck.

Before it grew too dark and too cold, Tío Joaquín would park in front of our little house in the village of Chubasco.

"Do you know the place?"

"Never been there, sorry."

"Not much, really, broiling during the day, freezing at night."

"Just like here." Nick grins.

"Much worse. But we liked it. Anyway, the town loved my sister and me, thought we were so sweet. In fact, everyone began calling us Las Hermanas Churros."

"Churro... like the pastry?"

"Papa was a baker who made the best Mexican pastries anyone had ever tasted. Even though we were little, we worked in his shop whenever we could."

Maria smiles. She can't remember the last time she reminisced about her childhood. It feels wonderful, especially with the owner of this great American ranch listening so attentively.

"After a morning helping Papa sprinkle sugary spices on so many treats, our hair often smelled like cinnamon.

"Uncle Joaquín would say that we were 'Delicious,' that we smelled like breakfast, and he wanted to eat us up.

"Our Auntie Lucinda had other ideas. 'You girls will be famous singers some day,' she would tell us. 'I guarantee it!'

"She called me, 'my practical girl,' because, she knew that whenever I had to solve a problem, even at the age of five, I would always try to come up with the most direct solution.

"Claudia, my older sister, wasn't that way at all. Aunt Lucinda would say, 'That girl is nothing but a dreamer.'"

Maria chuckles. "It's true.

"Claudia had visions of moving to the United States, opening a flower shop, and somehow becoming rich and famous. She talked about it all the time, even at the age of six, as though nothing could keep her from a wealthy life as a flower shop owner in America.

"In spite of our differences, Claudia and I did agree on one thing. We both loved Nacho. He was the most handsome boy in the village.

"At seven, he may have been a little chubby, but he always had a sparkle in his eyes. He could play the guitar, and sometimes he would accompany us when we sang.

"Also, he was always ready to laugh or tell jokes or make funny sounds. He could impersonate a whole backyard full of chickens and ducks and parrots and even donkeys. He'd do it during class. The whole room would burst out laughing, but teacher would get very angry and pretty soon Nacho would be sitting in the principal's office.

"We used to walk home from school together, Claudia, and Nacho, and I. We'd be talking, singing, always laughing, and always having fun. Unless we ran into Chato, that is. He was a kid with a pushed-in face... a real bully."

Nick nods at this and grimaces. He's known his share of bullies in his time. Unfortunately, he'd also been one for a while.

Maria doesn't try to interpret his expression. She just continues.

"Claudia and I didn't know why Chato hated Nacho so much, but he did. And he had a gang that was just as nasty as he: five ten-year-olds who would wait until we were on our way home. Sometimes Nacho had his arms around both of us, and we'd all be singing and laughing. Then the bullying would start.

"'Hey, sissy boy,' Chato would call from across the street, 'Why do you always play with girls?'

"'Not man enough to play with the big boys?' One of the other kids would add... probably Ramundo. He was Chato's second in command.

"'Come on over here, and let's see if you aren't just a big, fat, ugly girl yourself.'

"Nacho would stop in the street. His fists would clench. He'd try to get a mean look on that happy face. He couldn't do it. He would just look silly, and Chato's gang would laugh and start throwing things.

"Claudia wanted to step forward to defend Nacho, but I'd stop her. I knew that it would only make things worse. So, we'd look at each other, and then all three of us would just take off running.

"Sometimes Chato's boys would race down the opposite side of the street throwing rocks or cans or anything else they could get their hands on. We were lucky, the rocks never hit, but a big old soup can once bonked off Nacho's head. It spun him around and suddenly... he started laughing. He laughed so hard that the bullies didn't know what to think. They just stared at him for a moment, and then they looked at each other and then back at Nacho. Finally, they just ran off between the brightly painted houses.

"Claudia and I couldn't believe our eyes. Nacho was laughing. We'd look at his face. His forehead was cut. Blood spilled down into his eyes. Nacho laughed anyway.

"'This doesn't make any sense?' I said, and I pulled out a handkerchief and pressed it against the wound. 'Maybe that hit on the head made you crazy, Nacho.'

"He just kept smiling. And I remember this very clearly. He took the palm of his hand and hit his forehead with it.

"'Ka-BLAM!' he said, and he smashed his forehead again and doubled over laughing.

"'Ka-BLAM?' I asked. 'What kind of a word is that?'

"'Ka-BLAM,' he said again and smiled as though there were more to it.

"Then Claudia explained, 'It's the way the can sounded when it hit him on the head. It's a funny sound.'

"Nacho nodded and kept grinning.

"'But he's also smiling because he think's it also sounds like an idea popping into your head.' And then she started grinning too.

"'Si,' Nacho giggled 'Ka-BLAM!' and he smashed his bloody forehead with the palm of his hand again.

"I told them they were both crazy, but Nacho and Claudia just grabbed me by the arms, and we all headed home together.

"'Just forget it,' Claudia, told me. And Nacho added, 'Ka-BLAM!' It became his favorite phrase; he said it all the time after that... still does.

"What we found out later was that Chato watched the entire scene from farther down the road. He thought that Nacho was laughing at him, that the three of us thought he and his gang were fools. So, they decided they had to get even with us, embarrass us in front of the whole town... and they did... at the church fiesta."

#

"'What a lovely day!' I thought as I walked out of Sunday mass with Claudia and Mama and Papa. We were right behind Padre Carlos, and we all heard him tell Juan Pedro, this ancient old man who always served as altar boy, 'The Good Lord must want people coming to our fiesta from everywhere.'

"Old Juan was always very negative about everything, so he just said, 'Nice weather always makes me want to stay home.'

"The Padre smiled. He was always so happy about everything. 'No,' he said, 'this is the year that we finally raise enough money to fix the church roof.'

"'That roof is cursed,' said old Juan. He may have been right because so many people had worked so hard to raise money to get it fixed and yet it was still leaking when I left that town three years ago.

"The evening before, the men of the village had swept off the large cement court beside the church so that there could be an evening of dancing. They also swept off the little stage at the end of the dance floor. They built small booths, painted them, and decorated them with colorful streamers. And, by the time we walked out of the church, the fiesta was well underway.

"Families were already lining up to buy tacos and enchiladas and huevos rancheros prepared by the women of the village. The air smelled the way heaven must smell if the angels serve eggs and chorizo and tortillas on Sunday mornings up there.

"'Delicious,' I heard Padre Carlos say.

"'If you like stomach aches,' old Juan answered.

"Artisans from nearby towns had taken over many of the booths and sold leather bracelets, glassware, and other handicrafts.

"Directly across from the church entrance, Papa had set up his pastry stand, and it overflowed with the usual treats. Beside his booth, Aunt Lucinda had her own little business selling agua fresca and candy.

"Kids ran up and down the aisles between the booths, dodging the grown-ups who waited patiently in line for their breakfast.

"By now, Claudia and I were up on the little stage with Nacho. He had tuned his guitar and was ready to play. We had worked all evening with Mama and Tía Lucinda and Tío Rafael to decorate the stage with a little backdrop that showed a bright red wooden cart near a sunny country hillside. I had done the painting of the cart myself, and I was very proud of it.

"There were a lot of kids already standing in front of the stage. We weren't ready, so the adults were busy with other things... all off somewhere else.

"'Would you please play Cielito Lindo,' Little Cousin Veronica, called from down in the first row. She was even younger than I.

"Claudia smiled at me and nodded. 'But we're not ready,' I told my sister. 'There aren't any grown-ups here yet.'

"Claudia nodded. 'So what?' She said, and I could see that she was right. Nacho of course, just said, 'Ka-BLAM,' and grabbed his guitar.

"Our little cousin was eating a churro, and a lot of the powdery sugar had stuck to her face. She almost seemed to be wearing a beard made of sugar. Nacho began to play. Claudia and I began to sing, and everything felt wonderful. But before we could even get into the second verse, we saw Chato and his gang move in among the younger children. He snatched the churro away from Veronica and took a healthy bite. Then he passed the pastry to Ramundo, and he took a big bite too.

"'Give it back to me,' little Veronica shouted, and she tried to grab what was left of her treat, but Chato held it up over his head and made her jump for it.

"Claudia and I stopped singing. Nacho stopped playing. We just stared at Chato.

"The bully turned to the stage. 'Wanna make something of it, sissy boy?' he called to our friend.

"Nacho put down his guitar and went down from the stage. He stood toe-to-toe with Chato. The bully smiled and waited for a moment while Ramundo snuck behind Nacho and got down on his hands and knees right in back of our friend's legs.

"'Look out!' I shouted. But it was too late. Chato shoved Nacho, and he went toppling over backward, flipping over Ramundo, slamming into the edge of the stage and jarring the whole thing. Claudia and I fell over, and our little backdrop just tore apart. We had all worked on it for so long, and now it was destroyed.

"'Just look at the mess you made,' shouted Chato with a big smile.

"He and his gang laughed while Nacho turned red as he sat on the ground and Claudia and I began to sob. The bullies had a good long laugh, and finally turned to leave... but that's when they ran right into Padre Carlos.

"'I think it's time we did something about you boys,' the priest told them. 'There's a school in the big city that knows how to deal with kids like you. I'm going to talk to your parents about sending you there.'"

Back on the Melon Farm, Nick takes a sip of the coffee that has now grown cold. "So what happened?" he asks.

"They sent Chato and Ramundo off to the reformatory. They were there for seven long years. When they returned, Ramundo had turned really evil. Like he hated everyone. He even tried to burn down the church... which was silly. Churches don't burn."

"What about Chato?"

"He had entered the priesthood. We couldn't believe it. When he got back to town, Nacho planned to beat him silly. Nacho was much bigger than his old enemy by then.

"From a distance, we saw Chato get off the train carrying a valise. Padre Carlos ran up to him. We all crowded around. Nacho was trying to figure out how to get Chato alone. I think he planned to jump him as he went to get the rest of his luggage. Then Chato turned toward us, and we all saw that he was wearing a Roman collar. The bully had become a priest."

# Chapter Seven

Nick doesn't say a word for a long time. It's as if he's still thinking about everything Maria has said. Finally, he stands and gives her a look of admiration. "What a story. And you tell it well."

The couple stares at each other for a few more moments.

"Thanks for listening," Maria says as she reaches for his coffee cup. Her hands are trembling, and Nick realizes that reliving the events of the story has shaken her.

He hands the cup to her.

"Is there anything else?" Maria asks.

Nick looked confused. "I guess not... Only..."

"Only what?"

"I thought you were going to tell me about Juanito's father."

Maria stares at the handsome man for a long moment. Tears fill her eyes. "Oh yes," she finally answers. "Chato..."

"The priest?"

Maria nods. "He's the one."

"Really?" Nick can't seem to believe it. "And what happened to him?"

"I don't know. He was a priest, got forgiven by someone somewhere. They always are forgiven, aren't they? And then he was transferred out of our lives. I guess they thought I was what they like to call *an occasion of sin*."

Nick just shakes his head. "No," he says.

"The last I heard he was serving at the big cathedral in Mexico City."

"I'm sorry," says Nick.

"So am I," answers Maria.

#

Later that same evening, Maria has just picked up the dinner dishes. Juanito has inhaled a hearty portion of rice and beans and cheese, all wrapped in fresh corn tortillas supplied by the farm. He's made his way out onto the porch to play video games on his small game console, and now she is alone with Nacho.

The big guy reaches for a towel as Maria spills hot water into the sink, adds detergent and starts scrubbing.

"That Nick," Nacho begins. "I think he has a crush on you."

Maria shrugs. "He's a very handsome man. He could have any girl he wants. What would he do with me?"

"Marry you, have a bunch of kids, let you bring your whole family up here to live in wealth and comfort."

She grins crookedly. "Stop joking."

"Okay, if you're not interested in the gringo. I'll just marry you."

"Oh, Nacho," she coos. The big man grins. Stares at her intently for a moment, then smiles and adds, "Or maybe I'll marry Nick's sister."

"Britney... the singer?"

"I can accompany her on my guitar.

"I'll marry her and bring the whole family... you know the rest."

Maria is washing faster than Nacho can dry, trying to stay ahead of him. She drops another big plate into the little dish rack beside the sink.

"I'm not interested in importing my family across the border," she says finally. "All I want is to be left alone."

"Good luck with that," Nacho says. And then he suddenly grins. "Ka-BLAM!"

"Not another idea."

"Oh yeah. A double wedding: You and Nick, Britney and me."

"Nacho!"

"That girl loves me. I can tell."

"I'm sure she does," Maria adds. "All girl's love you. That's not the point. There are bad people here north of the border. People who just want to get rid of us."

"Britney doesn't think that."

"No, but she's a hot chica in a hot band that performs in a cantina full of tough guys. They'll chop you up into little pieces before they let you marry their sweetheart."

"Ka-blam?" Nacho asks. Then he looks away and puts all his energy into drying the dishes.

The phone suddenly rings, and Maria rushes over to answer it.

"Hola!" Maria answers. She hears a voice and gives Nacho a look that is half way between a smile and a sigh.

"Maria," her sister says through the phone. "It's me."

"Claudia? Is everything all right?"

"No! It's Uncle Joaquín. He was shot trying to cross the border."

"I know, Nacho told me."

"Nacho? How did you find him?"

"It's a long story he's here on the melon farm. He got a job."

"That's nice."

"It is. It was wonderful to see him again. But tell me about Uncle Joaquín, is he okay?"

"No, he's not. He's alive, but he has a terrible injury."

"Where?"

"Actually, he got shot in the... the nalgas!"

"His ass?"

"Yes, but it's worse than that. The bullet broke his hip, and he needs surgery if he's ever going to walk again."

"Take him to Central Hospital?"

"You know we can't afford that. Right now we are trying to figure out how to make the Americans pay for his surgery."

"Good luck with that!"


Nacho has finished drying the dishes. He spreads the damp towel over the lip of the sink and begins walking out the door. Suddenly he turns and shouts toward the phone. "Claudia, come see us. Maria and I are in love with wealthy Americans. They want to marry us, but we are too proud to let them." And he leaves.

"What was that all about," Claudia asks.

"You know, more of Nacho's fantasies. But he's well; somehow he managed to get across the border, and he looks... wonderful."

Claudia sighs. "We all should have made it. We paid good money to that coyote. I should be in Florida by now, working at a flower shop."

Maria shakes her head and wonders if she isn't the only sensible person in the whole family.

"He's just lucky, Claudia. And, what did I tell you about crossing the border illegally? If you wanted to come to the U.S., you should have come with me to work in the fields. But no, you were too good for that. You had to stay behind with your dreams and your lazy boyfriends, and now here are the results: poor Uncle Joaquín may never walk again. Nice going."

"Maria... I..." Claudia suddenly breaks into tears.

Maria can hear her sister sobbing on the other end of the line, and she starts crying too.

# Chapter Eight

Britney slinks between the patrons of the Lone Coyote Bar. She wears a spangly leather cowgirl vest over a partially unbuttoned blouse, a leather mini-skirt, and pink cowgirl boots. In her hand, she carries a microphone. She cozies up to one man and then another, tangling her fingers in the curly hair of a guy in a chambray shirt and then squeezing the stubbly cheek of an old cowboy who looks like he hasn't slept in weeks. All the while she's singing a sultry western ballad about how her man has left her, and she'll do anything to get him back.

Up on the small stage, the rest of Britney's Screaming Cowgirls band offers a sexy accompaniment.

Britney approaches the bar and recognizes her new friend, Nacho. He sits by himself nursing a beer, and when he sees her, his face lights up. She walks her fingers gently over his shoulders, then grabs him by the earlobe and gives it a friendly little twist.

Clayton Bailey, only a few seats further down the bar, leans back and glowers at her. Britney doesn't care. She belts out the torrid chorus, gives the crazy man a glare, turns, and struts up onto the stage to the wild applause of everyone in the place, especially Nacho.

"Thank you so much," she says. "But now, I'm afraid we need to take a little break. The girls need to do what girls need to do..." Everyone responds with a laugh. "And, well... I gotta pee. But we'll be back right soon, I promise."

She heads down toward the bar, walking almost directly toward Nacho. "Mi querida," he says raising his glass to her as she approaches. The girl winks at him but then walks right by him and takes a seat next to Clayton Bailey.

The murdering Texan is wild with jealous excitement. He immediately grabs Britney and practically spits his questions into her face.

"Why are you making eyes at the piece-a-shit Mex-can?"

"He's a fan is all," she giggles. "He likes my singing. I gave him a ride once. I think he's cute."

Bailey slouches back against the bar. "Yeah, that's right, they're all cute, those fuckin' Mex-cans... even the big, fat, ugly ones.

"But hey, girl, ain't I cute enough for ya?"

As he asks, he pulls his mask from his pocket, holds it up to his face, and gives her a horny grin.

Britney smiles. "Mmmmm," She coos sexily. "Hi ho, silver!" Then she leans forward and breathes into his ear. "You know that turns me on don't you masked man?"

His smile broadens. He closes his eyes contentedly. So the girl kisses him again, shrugs and slides over to Nacho.

"Hola hermoso," she flirts.

"Hola, gorgeous," Nacho answers.

"When ya gonna visit my shower again?"

"Whoa...." Nacho says in surprise. He starts to answer when a big hand suddenly grabs Britney and pulls her away from him. It's Bailey who seems incensed by their little exchange. He has a firm grip on each of Britney's arms. Nacho leans forward, his face right up next to hers.

51

"Excuse me, Señor," he says. "But that is no way to treat a lady."

Bailey let's go of the girl and makes his way to Nacho. He gestures over his shoulder at the singer.

"That flirt? She's no lady!"

You're right, Señor, she is not."

Britney looks at him in surprise, as if that's the last thing she ever expected him to say.

"She's an angel," Nacho continues, "and what you just did is even less of a way to treat an angel."

Britney smiles for a moment, but then she sees the look in Bailey's eyes.

"She's a slut! But she's my slut! And I'll treat her any way I like."

"I'm afraid not, Señor."

Bailey is tall, but Nacho is just bigger all around. Still, Bailey has the look of a madman.

"Who's gonna stop me?" he grunts.

Suddenly the voice of almost every man in the bar rings out: "I WILL!"

Britney gushes with joy; she's never felt so loved.

Bailey looks around. Men are sitting at all the tables and the bar. A small group of migrant workers sits at a little booth in the back. Farm hands both Mexican Americans and pure gringos occupy several of the tables. There are bosses, foremen, and even some ranch owners. They all have one thing in common: they all love Britney and won't let her get hurt. Bailey hears more than one unseen gun being cocked. He turns back to Nacho.

"I'll deal with you later, Pancho!"

"Soy Nacho," answers the big man. Then he adds his favorite word, "Ka-BLAM!" and slams the palm of his hand against his forehead in a gesture that's half way between a salute and a wave goodbye.

Bailey just looks at Nacho and shakes his head.

"You're crazier than I ever was," he says. Then he turns to Britney. "And *you* are on the wrong side now, bitch," and he marches from the bar.

"My hero," Britney coos, as she turns to Nacho and begins batting her eyes like the heroine in an old-time movie. She gives him a peck on the cheek and runs backstage.

Moments later she's with her band again. She nods to her girls, then approaches the mike, lowers her eyes, and after a minute, she takes a deep breath and begins to sing, "Quiéreme Mucho," a love song in Spanish, just for Nacho.

# Chapter Nine

That same evening, Claudia turns off the lights in her little apartment and climbs into bed with her Kindle reader. It's set to the first page of Don Quixote.

She's just getting into the story when there's a knock on her door.

"Damn, what time is it anyway?" she asks herself. But the little clock on her end table reminds her that it's only nine. She's allowed lots of time for reading.

"Coming," she calls as she gets up, grabs her robe, slides it over her shorty nightgown, and ties the belt around herself as she makes her way to the door.

"Who's there?" she calls.

"Tío Rafael," comes a muffled response. He sounds odd, distracted.

"What is it Uncle," Claudia begins as she swings the door open and then stops cold.

Rafael stands there looking half asleep. Antonio stands right behind him. His expression is full of concern and almost sorrowful. Beside Antonio is a slightly older man who looks so much like him that they could be brothers. This man's expression is so world-weary and disillusioned that it seems he could never have been happy.

Claudia responds at once.

"Come in. Come in," she says as she steps past her uncle, takes Antonio by the arm and pulls him inside. His partner and Tío Rafael follow.

"I'm sorry to be bothering you," says Rafael, but Antonio came to me about an hour ago and seemed very troubled. He insisted that he had to see you tonight."

"It's all right," answers Claudia, and then turning to the young man she asks, "What's wrong?"

"Oh, I'm sorry," he begins. "This is my cousin, Renaldo. I just picked him up in Tijuana and brought him here. I'll be driving him down to Tampico tomorrow."

Claudia smiles at Renaldo and nods.

"Señorita," he whispers.

"I thought you should hear his story," Antonio says. "Renaldo hasn't eaten in a while. I'm going to take him over to the café and get him something to eat. I thought you and Rafael might come with us and...."

"Nonsense," says Claudia. "I have plenty of food. There's pollo con mole and arroz y frijolitos from yesterday."

"That would be wonderful," Antonio answers. "If it isn't any trouble."

Claudia rolls her eyes but in a far kinder, gentler way than usual.

"Can we sit at your table?"

"Of course."

Antonio, Renaldo, and Rafael make their way to the big table in the center of Claudia's living room. They each take a seat.

"Wash up in the bathroom if you like," calls Claudia. She's already in the kitchen preparing the food.


In less than fifteen minutes Claudia has steaming plates of chicken with mole sauce and rice and beans for the men as well as mugs of beer. She also sets a big bottle of Tequila and a shot glass in front of Tío Rafael.

"Eat first and then you can talk," she says. And she watches with satisfaction as both men dig in and devour the food as though they hadn't eaten in days.

"I'm reading your uncle's book," Claudia tells Anthony.

"My uncle?"

"Miguel Cervantes, Don Quixote?"

Antonio grins. "You mean my great uncle. My great-great uncle."

"Your very great uncle," answers Claudia and the two of them laugh together. Tío Rafael chuckles as he sips his tequila. Renaldo tries to laugh too, but his look is so forlorn it embarrasses Claudia and makes her head back into the kitchen to get more beer.


At last the two men finish eating, Antonio stands and clears the table.

"Anything else I can get for you?" asks Claudia.

Antonio shakes his head. "It's time for you to sit and listen," he says. "My cousin has a story to tell."

Claudia nods and pulls a chair up beside Tío Rafael. He offers to pour her some tequila but she merely shakes her head, and so he downs another shot himself.


"When my cousin called me yesterday," Antonio begins, "I had a much different attitude than I do now. I thought you were crazy, Claudia. I thought your dreams were..." he shrugs, "Bullshit.

"But I guess I didn't know how good and how bad things could be in El Norte." He turns to Renaldo. "Tell the Señorita about your life there, cousin."

The older man nods and smiles wistfully. "Pretty sad stuff," he says. "But pretty incredible too. Twenty years of wonderful, and then nothing but shit."

Tío Rafael grunts in acknowledgement, toasts the air with his glass, and downs another shot.

"Tell us," Claudia says, and she leans in attentively as Renaldo begins his tale.

#

"I was only seventeen when I first went to the US," he says. "I crossed over then so easily it was like a walk down the avenue. I worked in the fields near San Diego picking flowers. I had so many friends... so much fun. We frequented the bars on the weekends, but during the week, Oh, Jesus, did we work.

"I was young; I was stupid. I'll admit it. One night when we were gathered in a bar, one of the other guys told us a story about how a bunch of local high school kids had made their way into the little encampment where his group lived. The gringo kids started breaking things, tearing up the place, just to make the point that we are not wanted here. And when the men tried to defend their property, such as it was, the high school kids fought back. Some of these kids were very big, must have been football players, and in the end, they had beaten several of our compadres badly.

"'The U.S. is not a safe place for us,' the guy told us. 'Get a gun. Own a gun; be able to defend yourself.'

"So, of course, like an idiot, I did," says Renaldo. "I got a gun. And then, when we were rounded up one night by the immigration services, I was deported because I had a gun. I was a criminal for nothing more than that."

"Madre de Dios," sighs Claudia. She reaches out and squeezes Renaldo's hand.

"That was my sin," he says. "That was my original sin... not my only sin of course."

"Of course not," says Tío Rafael.

"But God forgives, right?" asks Renaldo.

Claudia remembers her catechism, nods her head, and smiles.

"God is good. And the next time I entered America I vowed to be a better man. I went farther north, to Modesto California. I worked in the fields picking grapes. I was well behaved; I was a gentleman, and was rewarded with a gentleman's reward: a beautiful young woman came into my life.

"She was only seventeen then and worked beside me in the fields. Her name was Morena, and she came from farther south in Mexico. She had come with her father and her brothers who were also there. But this girl, ay... she worked harder than any of us. She was much younger than I, stronger too, with looks, oh Mother of God, that did not fade no matter how hard she worked. Even through all the chilly mornings and the boiling afternoons, she was always fresh and... delightful. She always had a kind word for everyone, a joyful expression on her face. She kept smiling at me... flirting with me I thought. What else could I do? I married her.

"And then to further show his goodness, God gave us the American dream: children, three of them all smart and bright, handsome, especially our daughter. If you called her a beautiful woman, you would not be wrong. She is in college now; at least she was the last time I saw her.

"Morena and I bought a house together. I was able to buy a truck. We drove to the mountains and camped as a family. My oldest son played soccer. I went to all the games, had picnics, American friends cheered beside us. We spoke English, paid taxes. We didn't mind; we owed it to that great land. There were so many good times. I got promoted; worked inside the plant, not out in the sun. Morena was able to stop work completely and raise our family.

"Then one day, after twenty years of the American dream, I went to work; it was just an average day, nothing special, nothing foreboding in the sky or the stars. There was nothing in the wind or the cry of the crows that perched as always on the wires outside the factory. I thought they were my brothers those crows, but they did not warn me.

"Inside our plant were officers from the immigration services. They were looking for a fellow from Brawley of all places. The guy, Sergio, had committed some kind of theft. And they were looking for him. I felt okay, I felt safe I had been a tax-paying American for twenty years, I had American children, a mortgage, and a loving wife who was on the board of the local parish for heaven's sake... and besides, God was good. But maybe my good God was on vacation on that particular day, because when La Migra could not find the man from Brawley, they decided to run the records on all the illegals in the plant... and there were so many of them. And one of them had been a sinner, had committed a felony just by owning a gun. He had been deported before.

"They took me then, packed me into a van; no one said a word in my defense. I was just deported. I did not see Morena again, or my American children. What I saw were the streets of Tijuana.

"I was alone with no money. I thought about crossing back, but I did not want to endanger my family. I knew that Morena was an illegal too. So I called Antonio here... a cousin I did not know, and he came and got me, brought me to your village, and here I am, a man without a country, or a family."

Claudia sighs and shakes her head.

"I called Morena as soon as I could. She is so terrified that she is unwilling to work. She does not go out of the house anymore; she has made herself a prisoner, and she is so lonely she tells me. Her brothers are helping pay the mortgage... but for how long?

"I've become convinced that I will never see my beautiful Morena again... or my children. When my daughter graduates from college, I will not be there. I cannot even afford to send her a gift. I will not see my boys play soccer... ever again; I will never go camping with my family or even sit around the table having supper with them. I am a sad man, my friends, but my wife and children are even sadder."

There is a moment of silence then.

Claudia can hear the facet dripping in the kitchen and realizes that she didn't turn it all the way off. She starts to get up but then, overcome with sadness, she just falls back into her chair.

"You were right Claudia," Antonio says suddenly. "It's time we teach those gringos a lesson!"

She winces. "But I...."

"I'm talking about standing up to the United States once and for all, ending their foolish sense of superiority."

"You'll never be able to do that, amigo," says Renaldo. "I've been there, I know."

"We can bomb them, we can find some symbol of America's senseless immigration policies and blow it to pieces."

Claudia stands slowly. She looks at Antonio with great disappointment. "Oh no," she sighs. "Mexicans are not terrorists."

Claudia walks toward Antonio. She takes his hands and smiles at him. "No terrorism. I want a world where the people of all nations respect each other."

Antonio sighs. "You and every dreamer who has ever lived. Respect is a worthy goal but impossible to achieve."

"Respect," sneers Tío Rafael. He belches loudly and quickly pours himself another shot of tequila.

Claudia stares at her uncle in disbelief for a moment and then turns back to Antonio.

"It's not an impossible goal."

"How can you achieve it then?"

Claudia closes her eyes and remembers an idea that first came to her as a high school girl reading about the shared history of Mexico and the United States. Could it be possible?

Suddenly the idea consumes her, and she says it with conviction. "We can start by TAKING BACK THE ALAMO!"

There is dead silence in the room. Even Tío Rafael holds his breath. Antonio stares at the young woman, and then he begins to laugh. It's not a kind laugh, or a pleasant one.

"And that's not terrorism?" he asks. "How the hell do you plan to take a national shrine without bloodshed?"

"Mostly OUR blood will be shed," adds Rafael.

Claudia laughs too. But it's not sarcastic or mean. It's sweet and full of hope.

"Creativity," she says, "trickery. We do not hold the Alamo; we take it just long enough to make a statement."

"Really?"

"The American Indians did something like that at Alcatraz," adds Renaldo. "They made their point."

"Did it have any lasting effect?" asks Claudia.

Renaldo sighs. "Not really."

"Okay, but I have always wanted a souvenir from the Alamo," cackles Tío Rafael. "A T-shirt maybe, or one of those little magnets people put on their refrigerators... for Tía Lucinda."

"Shush, uncle," says Claudia. Then her eyes brighten as she turns to Renaldo. "Thank you for your insight, Señor. So, we will need to do more than take the Alamo. We need a distraction to make people take us very seriously. We need them to think that we are preparing for war."

"Who is preparing?" mumbles Tío Rafael.

"The Mexican People."

"A people's war?"

"A people's army massing on the border, ready to invade."

"And while everyone focuses on the coming invasion...." says Antonio.

"A small band of Mexicans ride up in a little bus and takes over the Alamo," says Claudia. "We draw the attention of the press and get our message out."

"No bloodshed," says Antonio.

"But I want to kill Davy Crockett!" shouts Tío Rafael.

"Sorry uncle! He's already dead!"

"How about John Wayne then?"

"He's dead too."

"Oh," says the old man as he downs another shot of tequila. "Well, at least The Alamo is still with us."

# Chapter Ten

Britney Fleming has never been so angry. She dumps a big sack of cow manure into the back of her Jeep, slams the trunk lid, stalks around to the driver's side and gets in. Through the front windshield, she glares at the cause of her rage.

Walking out of the little church across the square on this bright Sunday morning is someone she thinks she's falling in love with. It's Nacho. Beside him strides a little boy of about five. Next to the boy is that woman Nacho introduced to her. She was in the cantaloupe fields the day she drove Nacho to her brother's ranch and got him the job.

What was the girl's name again? Britney asks herself.

"MARIA!" she shouts aloud. "I should have known what was going on right then."

She starts the Jeep and drives slowly through the people who are filing happily out of the church.

Britney has never been sure if people leaving church are happy because they feel blessed, or because they're glad that the service is finally over. Personally, she has never liked church or religion, mostly because of the things they keep telling her not to do. But none of that matters now. She feels like she might even be able to commit... TexMex-icide.

Nacho looks up, sees the familiar Jeep that rescued him when he first crossed the border, recognizes Britney, and waves. Only when he sees the look in her eyes does he fully understand why she's driving right toward him.

Heroically, he brushes Maria and her son behind him. He steps forward between them and the oncoming Jeep. He plants his feet, sticks out his chest, and just stands there challenging the cowgirl to run into him.

Britney slams on the breaks and comes to a stop just in front of Nacho.

The big man places his hand on the grill of the car as if to hold it in place, and then he walks around to the driver's window.

"Buenos días, hermosa. ¿Cuál es su problema?"

Britney glowers at him. "What's wrong? I'll tell you what's wrong! You! You are *so* wrong. You have a son, and a girlfriend, maybe even a wife."

Nacho stares at the girl who sang so sweetly to him in the cantina only a few nights ago. And then "Ka-BLAM!" it comes to him.

"No, silly," he says with that world-famous Nacho grin. "I have a friend...who is a girl... who has a son."

"That's what I said."

Nacho smiles patiently. "Yes, but no. I have a friend who has a son."

Britney glares at him.

"He's not MY son," he continues, "and she's not MY girl. I would like YOU to be my girl, Miha."

"Oh. Sorry," Britney sighs.

The singing cowgirl is silent for a moment; she bites her lip.

"Actually," he continues, "I think my friend is in love with your brother."

"Well maybe she has the hots for you too, pendejo."

Nacho answers with a shrug and a grin.

"But then I do too," she adds. "So, just get in, okay?"

Nacho looks up to see that a crowd has gathered around Maria and Juanito. They all look at him with concern: some crazed gringo cowgirl has almost run into him.

He walks back to Maria, says a few words, ruffles Juanito's hair, then goes to the passenger side of the Jeep and climbs in.

Britney leans across the seat and kisses Nacho. She makes it last; tongues are involved; it goes on and on. Nacho doesn't resist, and when the girl feels she has claimed him entirely, she drives off.

Nacho sucks in a deep breath, and sings out, "Ay, ay, ay, ay?" This time it's a question.


They drive on together. Nacho studies Britney who keeps glancing at him with both anger and regret. Nacho takes a deep breath not sure what to say. He gets a strange, confused look, wrestles with ideas, and finally murmurs, "I like your perfume."

The cowgirl giggles. "Really?"

"It reminds me of lazy days and sweet open fields."

"Is that right?" Britney giggles. "It's cow shit, Babe."

"That's the name of the perfume?"

Britney laughs. "That's the name of the principal ingredient in the manure that I have in the back of the Jeep."

"Oh," Nacho sighs. "Not so much like sweet fields, then." He grins as a new idea comes to him. "But, it will always remind me of you."


Britney pulls the little Jeep off the road beside a broad golden field. In the distance, a river gurgles slowly along. A big oak entertains extended families of birds. Half a dozen cows cluster under it, enjoying the tree's cooling shade.

"Catch me," the cowgirl calls as she pushes her door open, jumps into the field, and starts running across it.

Nacho takes off after her. He follows Britney down a slope to the bank of the river where he sees her bouncing on one leg while she pulls off her left boot and then, reversing the process, she takes off her right. She tosses the boots at Nacho, strips down to her undies, jumps into the river and dives deep underneath.

"Catch me, babe," she calls as she swims to the surface.

"I think I can do that," he calls as he dives in fully clothed.

Back on the road a big Ram pickup rumbles while a twitchy man dressed in baby blue cowboy duds looks on through binoculars. He witnesses the kisses that Britney and Nacho share in the water.

"Your life is over, Pancho," he murmurs, "and the girl's too... probably before the night ends."

#

Clayton Bailey now sits in front of his pickup on a lawn chair, a bottle of All American Beer between his legs. He doesn't know how long he's been sitting here. He remembers watching Nacho head down into the river and swim up to Britney. She turned to him, giggled, and kissed the fat bastard. Bailey had the guy in his sites, could have shot him dead, but he didn't do it. And he's been ashamed of himself ever since.

Bailey is looking across at the Mexican border now, a few miles away from the spot where he feels his girl betrayed him. (Funny though, she didn't feel that it was betrayal. He doesn't ask why.) He still feels angry, and bitter, and vengeful and somehow... sleepy. He uses his binoculars. His rifle is by his side, and he's ready to grab it and shoot any Mexican he spots trying to cross.

"Britney, babe, what they hell were you doing?" he sobs, and then shakes it off. His expression is resolute. He's killing a

Mex-kin tonight no matter how late it gets or how tired he becomes.

Suddenly, he's aware of a rustling behind him. There's a rush of motion, and then Bailey turns to see five bare-chested men in tights, wearing masks that fit snugly over their faces. They're rumbling toward him. The masks are of different primary colors: red, blue, yellow, green, black. There are patterns sewn into them: a starburst, a series of shapes that accentuate the wearer's eyes and mouth, a superhero design, and the features of wild animals. The men crouch as they come, as though they are going to spring at him. They are mostly big men; enormous, moving as though they are stalking their prey.

The giant in the yellow mask stalks up to Bailey.

"Buenos Dias amigo!" he growls.

Bailey almost jumps out of his chair. "Yes, Buenos Dias," he answers.

"Are you El Extranjero Solitario?"

Bailey eyes the big man blankly as though he has no idea what he is asking.

"Are you the Lone Stranger?"

Bailey's fingers slowly curl around the top of his rifle even though he knows that he won't have time to raise it before the men are on him. Still, it allows him to feel a little safer. And so he answers.

"Yes, I am. And who are you fellas?"

The man in the yellow mask bows dramatically. Curley strands, sewn into the facial covering resemble the mane of a lion. The nose and eyes of the jungle cat are painted on. "We are los luchadores, famous wrestlers from Mexico," he growls.

Bailey looks from one man to the other. They are moving closer, surrounding him.

"Why are you here?"

The wrestlers cock their heads, look at each other then back to him, and grunt disapprovingly.

"If I may ask," Bailey adds quickly.

"For an especial event," answers the man in the lion mask.

"And where is your mask, amigo?" questions a heavier, darker skinned wrestler whose mask has gray hair and teeth sewn into it so that it makes him resemble a coyote.

Bailey's terror fades a little as he reaches into his shirt pocket and finds his mask. But when he pulls it to his face, he's horrified to see that it's all white and in the style of the Mexican wrestlers, but this mask has a painted hole for a nose and hollow eyes that make it look like a skull. He puts it on anyway, feeling as he does that it is what he will soon become... a dead man.

"I am El Leon," growls lion mask, and he leans back, twists his hands into the shape of claws, rakes the air with them, and roars.

"I am Coyote Gordo," says the wrestler who asked about Bailey's mask. Gordo stalks forward growling like a beast, sniffing around Bailey in a way that makes the Texan feel very threatened. Coyote Gordo grins slyly. But the look is not reassuring.

"This is Pepito El Bonito," rumbles Lion Mask as he points to the only small man in the group. He's about four feet tall, dressed in blue and red. He wears a cape and flexes his muscles to show off arms that could rival Superman.

"This is Garapata and Gara Nalgas," continues Lion Mask, and the two other Mexicans strut and pose like wrestlers before the main event.

"Glad to meet you all," says Bailey nervously.

"I don't think so," hisses Garapata.

"Amigo, are you a man?" queries Gara Nalgas as he moves forward and glowers down at the Texan. The wrestler's breath is rank, and Bailey wants to turn away, but he doesn't dare.

"Are you a dangerous and mean man?" asks Lion Mask.

Bailey jumps to his feet almost involuntarily. "Yes," he shouts proudly. "I am!"

"And you hate Mexicans? Si?" hisses the coyote.

Bailey steps forward, "Well not really. You see...."

"You shoot with your gun and try to kill them," says Pepito El Bonito. "Yes?"

"Well, I'm just trying to...."

"To what?" grumbles Garapata like some kind of ogre.

"To...."

Lion Mask drops a gnarled hand onto Bailey's shoulder, "We are proud Mexicans, ourselves, amigo."

"And we are here to kick your ass," says Pepito El Bonito cheerfully. But his look is not cheerful. It's menacing.

"No, wait!" Bailey cries.

"We do not wait, Amigo!" growls the lion and he suddenly reaches forward with his claws and rips the skeleton mask completely off of Bailey's face.

Pepito barrels directly into the Texan's chest and knocks his chair over backward.

Garapata lifts Bailey to his feet just in time for Gara Nalgas to drive a fist right into his eye.

Bailey falls to his knees and throws his arms across his face for protection as the five wrestlers now begin to beat him mercilessly.

"Oh, No! No! No!" Pleads Bailey.

"Si! Si! Si! Amigo!" growls the lion, as the beating continues.

#

It's dead black night! A gunshot suddenly wakes Clayton, and he finds himself sprawled on the ground beside his Truck. His rifle lies in front of him. His chair has tipped over backward. He touches his face expecting to find nothing but bruises and cuts, but there are none... and no pain. He's sweating and breathing heavily.

"What just happened?" he asks the night air, as he looks out onto the horizon and sees a small band of Mexicans making their way into Texas.

"Nightmare," says Bailey with a half smile. I squeezed the trigger in my sleep, fired the gun and toppled over backward in my chair.

He struggles to his feet.

"Maybe not," someone seems to whisper.

Bailey freezes for a long moment.

"Who said that?"

"Must be the breeze," Bailey thinks as he packs his rifle and chair into the back of his truck and gets ready to head for home.

"Must be the breeze."

# Chapter Eleven

It's evening at the Faithful Chicken Bar in Chubasco, Sonora Mexico. Antonio, Claudia, Tío Rafael, and Padre Carlos sit together in a little booth near the rear. Each of them has a large glass of beer. Rafael's is already half gone.

"So then, here it is," says Antonio as he unfolds a map of the US/Mexican border.

"And there's the wall," adds Padre Carlos reaching forward and drawing several rough lines with his pen.

"It's only there to keep out los gabachos," mumbles Rafael.

"I'm afraid not," says Padre Carlos, "It's there to keep Mexicans in."

"No wall can keep out men and women who need to earn a living and support their families," says Rafael.

"Wanna bet?" asks Antonio.

The two men stare at each other for a long moment.

Claudia shakes her head.

"No point in bickering," she says. "There's no time. There are too many problems we need to solve. Massing an army on the border, sneaking into Texas to seize the Alamo, where will we get the men and equipment?"

Antonio smiles confidently, "When the Mexican people learn of our plans, they will come from everywhere... even the remote villages. They'll join us and march beside us. They won't have training, but they will give us numbers, and the gringos won't dare to attack so many."

"Who's the dreamer now?" asks Claudia with a smile.

Antonio shrugs.

"So then our first step is get the word out," says Claudia. "If our peasant army is at the border, we can taunt the Americans as they build the latest section of their ridiculous wall. We will draw cameras and newscasters from all over the world."

"The loco American Presidente will become even crazier," says Tío Rafael.

"He'll tweet out all kinds of hate," laughs Antonio.

"And," adds Claudia excitedly, "as all of this is going on, a small band of warriors can sneak in Texas and take the Alamo... but only for a moment."

Antonio's smile broadens... "As a gesture."

"As a publicity stunt!" says Padre Carlos.

"Si Se Puede!" growls Tío Rafael, and he plunges his knife right into the center of the map... right into the big white star that indicates the location of The Alamo.


"But what about the logistics?" whispers a voice from behind their little booth. Claudia and the others turn to see Emilio standing there. Once again he's holding a bottle of Tequila.

"Why are you drinking that sludge?" he asks gesturing to the beer. He moves forward and puts his bottle on the table.

"We want to think clearly," mumbles Tío Rafael.

"You have never thought clearly in your whole life, old man," says Emilio.

"We don't need your help," says Padre Carlos. "Didn't I make that clear?"

"Perhaps," the dark man answers. "But I think you DO need me."

Claudia crosses her arms defensively. "No, Señor. We have our own ideas."

"I'm sure your ideas are excellent, beautiful lady," says Emilio. And now he nudges his way into the booth beside her. "But logistics are important too. For example, HOW will you get the word out, and exactly WHERE will you mass this people's army?"

Antonio eyes Claudia uncertainly.

"Will they need training and discipline of any kind, or will these peasant warriors just show up and miraculously know how to be soldiers?

"Who will command them, who will organize them?"

Claudia lowers her eyes for a moment and looks at her hands. "Well...."

Emilio begins pouring shots of tequila and passing them around.

Rafael downs his as soon as it comes his way.

Antonio eyes Claudia for a moment then shrugs and takes a sip.

"The answer to the first question, HOW," says Emilio, "is through some kind of well-established communication network. As for the WHERE... the answer could be the old deserted mining town of Los Lomas. It's right here." And he jerks Rafael's knife out of the table and slams it back through the map at a place where Padre Carlos's pen marking stopped to indicate a gap in the wall.

Claudia looks down at the spot, then up at Padre Carlos. He studies her carefully and then shakes his head. Emilio ignores him.

"My brother currently owns the property, but I might be able to persuade him to make it available to you. Just as he may be able to use his well established communication network to get your word out. Just as he might be willing to supply seasoned military leaders who can train your people's army."

"Why would he do that?" asks the priest.

"Why do you think, Padre?" Emilio answers as he raises his own shot glass to his lips. "He's a businessman, but he is also a patriot. He shares the same frustrations and hopes as you do."

"He shares our hopes," murmurs Claudia. "Just who is he?"

Emilio smiles. "Why friends. I thought you knew. Padre Carlos does. My brother is El Rey del Frijol."

"The King of Beans?" asks Claudia.

"Of course, Señorita. Who else?"

"Owner of the largest bean fields in all of Mexico," says Antonio.

"Master of a food produce empire," says the Padre as he reaches for the glass and takes a slow sip. "But he's a very shrewd man who has never been known to trust his brother."

"Oh, he trusts me now," says Emilio. "Believe me. I have recently brokered several profitable deals for him, and he's actually become a big fan of mine."

"But won't our efforts hurt his business?" asks Antonio. "I would think he would prefer to maintain the status quo."

Emilio smiles. "Perhaps Claudia and her army are the vanguard of a new age, muchachos. It is always good to be in on the start of new things. Is it not? We give you support, we ease the tensions at the border and soon products and services flow more freely. Everyone is happier. Mexican workers find jobs in the fields of America. Citizens of the United States develop even broader tastes for Mexican food. They buy more beans, what could be better?"

"So The King of Beans would sponsor an army?"

"I'm sure I can convince him to do it," adds Emilio. "WE would sponsor Claudia's Army. SHE would be the face of the coming age."

Padre Carlos shakes his head in doubt. But when he turns to Antonio he sees that the young man's eyes are sparkling. He's thrilled with the idea.

The Padre turns to Tío Rafael who raises his glass in a small personal toast. "Si Se Puede!" he murmurs happily.

To his right Claudia looks concerned and confused but then she sees Antonio's look and she too raises her glass.

"Why am I the only one here who doesn't trust this guy," the priest mumbles to himself.

# Part Two

# Chapter Twelve

Nancy Malone stands in front of the dairy case at the local Quickie Mart. When did milk get so complicated, she wonders: soymilk, almond milk, non-fat milk, low-fat milk, skimmed, whole? Not that she ever buys it. Her housekeeper Miranda does. But hardworking hubby Chuck wants some milk for tomorrows breakfast, and since the poor guy gets up at 5:30 AM Nancy is stopping on her way home from the country club to pick up a carton.

Nancy wears well-pressed Bermuda shorts and a thin cotton blouse with little hearts embroidered everywhere. Beside her, her four-year-old son Johnny tugs on her fingers.

"Mommy," he says, "Look at that guy."

Nancy glances across the convenience store and sees a big man, clearly a Mexican laborer of some kind, standing at the counter.

Nancy instinctively pulls her son a little closer. She knows how eager the boy is to meet new people.

"Don't talk to strangers, Johnny," she whispers.

Little Johnny hasn't learned his lesson because he immediately shakes free and heads over to the counter where the man is buying the bag of corn chips. It's Nacho.

"Hey, mister," Johnny says with a wave.

Nacho smiles and waves back. "Hey, kid."

The big Mexican dumps a pocketful of change onto the counter and smiles at the pimply young clerk working the cash register.

"For the bag of Nachos?" asks the clerk.

Nacho nods enthusiastically and then watches the pimply kid count out the cost of the chips.

"Uh, you gave me a little too much change," says the clerk as he pushes four quarters back to Nacho. The big guy scoops them up and shoves them back into his pocket. Then, he tears open the bag of chips, pushes several into his mouth, turns, and walks down the aisle chewing as he goes.

Johnny follows. He's dressed in cargo pants, crocks with socks, and a camo t-shirt. "Hey, mister, those any good?" asks Johnny.

Nacho turns. He's in the soft drink section now, standing between cartons of cola and other beverages stacked as high as his shoulders. Nacho smiles at the kid and suddenly calls out Ka-BLAM! as he quickly holds out the bag of chips.

"What do you think?" he asks.

"Really? Can I have one?"

"Of course," Nacho answers and pushes the bag even closer.

"Gee, thanks," says the kid. He reaches into the bag and pulls out a handful. "I love nachos."

"Me too," says the big man. "Especially because my name is Nacho."

"Just like the chips?"

"That's right."

The kid smiles at Nacho admiringly and then reaches into the bag and pulls out another handful. "Do you own the company?"

Nacho laughs, "I wish."

The kid munches the chips, but now he looks confused.

"Is your picture on the bag?"

Nacho looks at the bag of chips, studies the back and front, and then turns it sideways. "No. No picture of me."

Johnny shrugs.

"Ka-BLAM," Nacho repeats as he flips the open bag toward the kid who quickly grabs another handful.

"Thanks for the nachos," he says, and then turns and runs down the aisle toward his mother who is still standing at the dairy case.

"That nice man gave me some chips," Johnny tells his mother. She eyes Nacho suspiciously, but then she gives him a half smile and pulls her little boy closer to her.

"You shouldn't talk to strangers, Johnny."

"I know but he was nice, and he gave me some chips."

"You shouldn't take food from strangers either."

"But Mom, he said, Ka-BLAM!"

Nancy rolls her eyes. "Wonderful dear. But it's still not wise. Now, stay close. I'm almost finished here."

Nacho watches the scene play out and then sighs. The mother's distrust bothers him, but he understands that's the way mothers are. For a second he misses his mother, and his childhood, and his hometown. Then he turns and almost runs right into Andy Meyers.

"Well, what have we here?" asks Meyers.

"Someone who's been sharing his chips, eh," answers Toronto.

The skinny teen peers out at Nacho from behind Meyers' heavy frame.

"Why would a big Mex-can share his food with a little kid," asks Meyers, "A white kid at that?"

Toronto considers the question. "I don't know."

"Maybe he wanted to kidnap the kid and hold him for ransom?"

"That seems unlikely," says Toronto.

Meyers frowns. "Well, just maybe it *is* likely. Yeah, that could be it. Anyway, we'd better tell the boss."

Nacho just shakes his head in disbelief, but then Clayton Bailey walks up behind him and taps him on the shoulder. Nacho turns, and Bailey glowers at him.

"Well, hello there asshole. Stolen anyone else's girlfriend lately?"

Nacho holds his ground. "Girls like Britney cannot be stolen, Hombre."

"Oh yeah? Why else would she prefer you ta me then, scumbag?"

Nacho grins. "Maybe I'm prettier than you are."

Bailey crosses his eyes as though puzzling over the idea. Then he shakes his head frantically. "Not a snowballs chance in Mexico, boy. Now, drop those chips and face me like a man."

Nacho doesn't feel threatened. "Are you afraid that I will use these chips to harm you?"

"Don't be ridiculous," Bailey answers. "Let's just step outside."

"And what will we do out there?"

"I'll punch your face in, you sack of shit. You're trying to steal a sweet, innocent, white girl."

Nacho smiles. "I told you, she cannot be stolen. But you are right. She is sweet, and she is very fair. But as for innocence...."

"What are you saying, creep?"

"I'm saying that Señorita Britney is a fully grown, experienced woman who can make her own choices. She does not belong to anyone, not me, not you, not anyone."

"I don't think so," growls Bailey. "After we get through with you, she's going to belong to me completely."

He turns to Meyers and adds, "If I have to tie her up and brand her."

Then he's back mumbling at Nacho, "No more singing in that stinkin' café either. You've filled her head with a bunch of

Mariachi bullshit. And it's time for us to give the girl a re-education."

Myers snickers, but Toronto looks very concerned.

"That is, after we make you pay."

He pulls his mask from behind his back and holds it in front of his eyes. "The Lone Stranger is here to collect."

"You can't take me one-on-one, can you, Hombre?" Nacho asks. "You need your buddies to hold me while you beat me up?"

Bailey smiles, tucks the mask back into his pocket, and pulls out his cell phone. "Glad you mentioned 'buddies'," he says. "Because now you really are toast, amigo."

He eyes Meyers. "Just calling for backup," he says. He punches in a number, and Nacho's smile fades.


A moment later a huge black Ford 4 X 4 roars into the parking lot outside and five men pile out of it.

"Grab him now!" Bailey shouts, and Meyers rushes Nacho and wraps his arms around the big Mexican.

"Hey there," Nancy Malone suddenly calls out. "Leave that man alone." Her voice is stern, like a schoolmarm addressing a class full of naughty boys.

"Yeah, leave him alone," echoes her son.

"You don't have to worry, Miss," says Bailey, "We've got the situation under control, here."

"No," shouts Nancy. "Don't you hurt him!"

"It's okay, Lady. Everything's all right. We'll get this dirty..."

"Uncle Stranger," says Toronto, "You don't really want to do this, do you?"

Bailey grins. "Does a Mexican shit in the desert?"

"Not funny, Hombre," Nacho says as Meyers holds him. "Did you ever try and wipe your ass with the pad of a prickly pear cactus?"

Bailey looks at Nacho incredulously.

"Oweeee, does it hurt."

"Not like the hurt we're about to put on you, asshole," grunts Meyers.

"Get him out into the parking lot," says Bailey just as the five men from the huge Ford begin to move toward the Quickie Mart.

"STOP IT!" calls Nancy Malone.

Bailey turns to her in anger. "Will you just shut the fuck up, bitch!"

Nancy steps back, pulls her son to her, and holds him. Her face twists into a mask of disbelief.

"Don't let them hurt the nice man, mommy," Johnny says.

"I'd better create a diversion," says Toronto as he snatches the bag of nachos away from the fat man and takes it up to the counter. "Another bag a these, eh," he says to the skinny checkout clerk. "And a bottle a Thunderbird wine."

The clerk, who can barely be twenty-one, focuses on the kid and does his best to ignore Bailey and Meyers as they hustle Nacho out into the parking lot.

"Got some ID?" he asks Toronto.

He's turned his back to the window and doesn't see Bailey take a baseball bat from his truck. The five new arrivals cluster around Nacho, who stands there facing them."

Nancy Malone reaches for her purse, pulls out her cell phone, and starts punching in a phone number.

"Yes, I need to speak to the police," she says.

"Oh, Jesus," moans Toronto as he grabs the chips and rushes out into the night.

"Uncle Stranger, no," he shouts, "Don't kill him. Please. That woman is calling the cops. There are witnesses to all this."

He breaks through the crowd to see Nacho bloodied and beaten. Meyers holds him as the others line up and each delivers a hard punch to his gut. The Lone Stranger stands there holding the bloody baseball bat. He drops it and slams a roundhouse right that jerks Nacho's face to the side and splatters teeth and blood onto the pavement.

Suddenly, police sirens cut through the night.

"Motherfucker!" screams Bailey as he rushes to the door of the convenience store.

"If any of you breathe a word of this to the cops... or anyone... I will personally see to it that you never breathe again. Understand? Now get the fuck out of here."

Nancy, the clerk, even the little boy nod helplessly. Bailey spins away from the store, and rushes to his truck. He and those in the big Ford peel out just before the police arrive. Nacho lies on the pavement very close to death, a broken jaw, shoulder, ribs, and several missing teeth.

The checkout clerk rushes out through the back of the store leaving all the doors open as he does.

"We have to go," calls Nancy as she tries to drag her son along.

"But mommy, the nice man is hurt," screams little Johnny.

"It's okay, baby. The police are here. They'll take care of him. We have to go."

And the woman whose phone call saved Nacho's life lifts her son and carries him out through the back to the parking lot where her Mercedes offers reassuring warmth and quiet.

# Chapter Thirteen

"What a sermon," says Tío Rafael. "Padre Carlos was inspiring today."

"He looked twenty years younger too," adds Tía Lucinda. "Like the novice who first came here so many years ago."

They are walking slowly from the church on this bright Sunday morning, and only as they move out into the plaza do they become aware of the excitement in the crowd. Everyone is energized by the padre's words. They are smiling, talking gaily, and suddenly feeling full of hope. No one is more excited than Claudia. Her white Sunday dress almost makes her look spiritual, like some kind of angel... a warrior angel though. The set of her jaw confirms that.

Antonio walks along beside her. He can't stop looking at her. She is so gorgeous, so inspiring, he thinks, and he vows to do anything necessary to help her reach her goals.

"I've never heard Padre Carlos speak like that," murmurs Claudia. "He was just so... so *visionary*."

"He shares your ideals," says Antonio.

"Yes, but he expresses them so well. I could never...."

Antonio stops. They have crossed the street and are standing in a little park.

"You can express anything you want to," he says.

"But he's eloquent."

"You can be too."

She blushes and smiles sweetly. "You obviously haven't been listening to me lately, sir."

"More than you know, ma'am," he answers.

"And what have I said?"

"You tell me," answers Antonio, and he takes Claudia around the waist and lifts her up onto a small flat bench so that she's standing there looking down at him.

Then, smiling playfully, he asks. "Just what is your vision, Claudia?"

For a moment, the young woman seems anxious. She stares nervously down at her hands as though she's a schoolgirl asked to deliver the graduation address. And then she looks up at Antonio. He smiles at her and nods expectantly.

"I think it's time," she begins softly. And then she stops.

"Yes?" Antonio encourages.

"Well, it's more like, *the time is approaching.*"

"Good. Okay."

"For us to act together... with COURAGE."

"Very good," responds Antonio, and Claudia's eyes begin to sparkle.

"WE MUST MAKE OUR COUNTRY AND OUR NEIGHBORS TO THE NORTH TAKE NOTICE. WE HAVE AN IMPORTANT MESSAGE FOR EVERYONE."

"Yes," answers Antonio. "And that message is...."

"RESPECT FOR HUMANITY!"

"Amen!"

Claudia now begins to speak much more loudly, to project her words not just to Antonio but to others who are passing through the little park as well.

"WE HAVE GROWN TIRED OF FACING DANGER AT OUR BORDER... GENERATION AFTER GENERATION."

The churchgoers take notice and begin to approach Claudia. They gather around her.

"DOWN WITH HATE AND CORRUPTION... ON BOTH SIDES."

"YES!" shouts a young man at the edge of the crowd.

"PRESIDENT DE LA PALMA ALTA AND PRESIDENT DRIVEL MUST BE MADE TO UNDERSTAND WE ARE WILLING TO SACRIFICE OURSELVES TO END THIS LONG HISTORY OF MISUNDERSTANDING AND VIOLENCE... SACRIFICE EVEN OUR WELL BEING... EVEN OUR LIVES!"

The crowd now begins to buzz. More and more people gather: men, women and children, those from the church and others who just happen to be out on that Sunday morning. A very professional woman wearing horned rim glasses and a red sweater moves purposefully up through the crowd.

"LONG LIVE OUR LADY OF GUADALUPE AND THE PROTECTION SHE BRINGS US!" shouts Claudia. "WE WILL SOON CREATE A NEW ORDER FOR OUR WORLD, AN ORDER THAT WILL BENEFIT *ALL* THE PEOPLE. WE CAN DO IT!"

"Si Se Puede!" respond many of the older men in the crowd. Some have tears in their eyes as they look at this latest incarnation of the spirit of Mexican fighting womanhood.

"Adelita, has returned," Tío Rafael whispers to his wife. And at that very moment the breeze picks up and begins swirling Claudia's long black hair around her face. She breathes deeply with excitement, puffs out her chest, almost taking on the posture of a super-hero.

"REMEMBER THAT THE HISTORY OF *BOTH* OUR COUNTRIES HAS ALWAYS REQUIRED SACRIFICE!"

"WE MEXICANS HAVE KNOWN PAIN AND STRUGGLE FROM THE VERY BEGINNING."

The crowd cheers.

THE TIME FOR *THIS* GENERATION'S SACRIFICE HAS COME!"

They cheer even louder.

"IT WILL LEAD TO BETTER LIVES FOR EVERYONE."

The woman in the red sweater has been holding up her iPhone as Claudia speaks, recording everything she says, and the way that the crowd responds to her. At just the right moments she stops her recording, snaps a few iPhone photos, then goes back to recording.

"WE MUST FACE THE AMERICANS AT THE BORDER. WE MUST STAND UP TO THEIR CRAZY PLANS. IF NECESSARY WE MUST FORM AN ARMY... STARE THEM IN THE EYES. TELL THEM *THERE WILL BE NO WALL!*"

The words echo through the crowd; it almost becomes a chant. "There will be no wall... there will be no wall."

"THIS IS THE ONLY WAY TO JOURNEY INTO THE FUTURE," Claudia continues. "AND THAT FUTURE IS ONLY DAYS AWAY!"

The crowd erupts into wild cheering. There are now dozens of people gathered around Claudia. Some begin chanting 'Si se Puede,' others cry, 'There will be no wall,' over and over again.

Claudia stands there exhausted from speaking. She nods to the crowd, waves to some, and blows kisses to others. But she's gasping for breath, sweating from the effort and yet looking more magnificent than ever because of it. She now stares out beyond the crowd as all visionaries do, eyes fixed on some distant object.

Antonio jumps up onto the bench beside her. He leans close to her, chuckles, and whispers, "Too bad that you're just *not* very good at describing your vision?"

Claudia is so energized that she doesn't even hear him. But she lets him hold up her hand like some champion prizefighter. The crowd cheers.

"SI SE PUEDE," shouts Antonio.

"SI SE PUEDE," they answer.

# Chapter Fourteen

Dust swirls across the big parking lot outside the Santa Teresa Medical Center in Mesa Texas. Britney Fleming's jeep roars through the circular driveway and, with the sounds of squealing brakes and burning rubber, comes to a lurching stop in one of the emergency parking spaces.

The singing cowgirl jumps down from behind the steering wheel, rushes across the entryway, and bursts inside. The main lobby of the hospital is vast and antiseptic. Dispensers of hand sanitizer flank the sliding glass doors. Concerned families (some with young children, others with members in wheelchairs or casts, still others who are elderly and somewhat disoriented) occupy the cushy chairs beside tables full of magazines.

Across the lobby rotunda, a long information desk offers help and direction to new arrivals. Britney marches up to it and whips off her cowgirl hat. Her beautiful blond hair is tangled with neglect. Her daisy dukes are riding too low on her hips. Her cowgirl boots are rumpled. The only thing neat about the girl is her starched white cotton blouse. But even this shirt is buttoned unevenly, as though she put it on way too quickly.

"Nacho?" she asks frantically. "Where can I find him?"

Mrs. Miller, the sweet looking receptionist with blue/gray hair and wire-rimmed glasses, looks at the girl in confusion.

"The guy who was beaten so severely," says Britney.

"Oh, you mean Mr. Francisco Alfredo Gonzales Gonzales Gonzales?"

"That's right, three Gonzales. Has he shown any signs of recovery?"

Mrs. Miller pulls down her glasses, looks above the rims and checks her computer screen.

"He's still in guarded condition, I'm afraid," she says, "But the doctor is with him now. Are you family?"

"I'm his uh..." Britney stops and considers. What is she to Nacho? "I'm his *cowgirl*," she announces proudly.

Native Texan, Mrs. Miller understands fully. "Very well then," she says. "Take the elevators to your right... up to the third floor, Room 328." And she slides a pass to the girl who grabs it quickly, turns, and jogs toward the elevators.


Moments later, Britney charges into room 328, her boots clattering loudly across the linoleum. She sees Maria talking to someone. 'Doctor Johnson,' his nametag announces. They both turn toward the girl as she slows and walks more carefully into the room. Lying on the bed, attached to half a dozen monitoring devices, eyes closed, a mass of bruises, is Nacho.

"Oh God," sighs Britney, and she moves slowly toward him. She reaches forward and takes his hand.

"Oh Nacho," she sighs. Then she turns to the doctor. "He's unconscious?"

Doc Johnson nods his head. "He was beaten so badly."

"Those bastards," curses Britney and her eyes darken. "I'm going to have to do something about this."

"The police were here earlier," Maria says. "No one has been willing to identify the assailants. There were witnesses. But no one will come forward."

"I'll come forward," says the cowgirl. "Everyone knows who did it; it was Clayton Bailey, that moron who calls himself the Lone Stranger."

"They say he has an alibi," whispers Maria.

Britney glances back at the young woman and eyes her up and down. "Yeah right."

She turns back to Nacho. The doctor brings her a chair. She sits, still holding his hand. She lowers her head, and her lips move silently in prayer.

"Blessed Mother of God," the girl whispers, "Please intercede. Give this handsome hunk back to me. Let him awaken with all that wonderful stuff that (you know) I love so much... his sense of humor and his joy, and those wonderful kisses." She glances back at Maria and the doctor who immediately turn their eyes away in embarrassment.

Britney reaches forward and squeezes Nacho's biceps. "Please keep him strong: These powerful arms that make me feel so safe when they're holding me.... those delicious lips that taste like hot salsa when they're kissing me." She leans forward and kisses Nacho hungrily.

"I've been such a fool flirting with all those other men when it's only Nacho, sweet Nacho...."

She turns to Maria. There are tears in Britney's eyes, but she still stares accusingly at the other woman.

"I'm so jealous of you," she says. "You grew up with him. You saw his sweet smile all your life."

Maria shrugs. She's starting to cry herself now. She glances over at Nacho and his eyes suddenly pop open. Britney doesn't notice. She's not looking at his face.

"Oh my baby," says the girl as she takes Nacho's hand, pulls it toward her breasts and holds it firmly against them.

"These hands were so hot and sexy when they were on me. Mmmmm."

Nacho's eyes grow wide. He smiles. Maria starts to move toward Britney but Nacho shakes his head slightly, and she stops.

"Oh Nacho, if I could have you back with me," the girl continues, "I would change everything. I would stop flirting with all the men in the bar. I'd even stop singing there if that's what you want. I'll gladly marry you, become your wife, and give you dozens of little niños."

Nacho smiles, nods, but then feels the strain and stops with a grimace.

"I know you would hesitate, sweet Nacho. I know you would be concerned about the dangers of my marrying an illegal. What will the townspeople say?"

Nacho frowns and shakes his head.

"I don't care. You were always so strong, so wise, so handsome, Nacho."

The wounded Mexican is almost bawling. But Britney still doesn't look up.

"What a good man you are. What a good, good man."

Nacho is now nodding in agreement, but Maria and the doctor are starting to smirk.

"Oh, Nacho, come back to me, please," continues Britney, "I will do anything you ask. I will be your wife, your lover, your mistress, your guardian, your own personal cowgirl, your cook, your humble servant."

"Is anyone writing this down?" asks Nacho suddenly, and Maria can't help but burst out laughing.

"Nacho?" whispers Britney. "You've come back to me." And she looks up, sees that he's awake, and lunges for him. She wraps her arms around the wounded man, and only the doctor's quick efforts can restrain her and save Nacho's body from greater damage.

"You don't want to hurt him now," says the doc.

Britney pulls back, wipes the tears from her eyes, and grins.

"Hey, you're cute," she says to the doc and then catches herself. She shrugs and turns back to Nacho. "How much of that did you hear, mi amor?"

"Uh, most of it... I think," he says. "It was very... uh... can I say... accurate."

"Yes it was," says Britney. "But I have to tell you that the evil men who hurt you are still out there."

Nacho shrugs as though it doesn't matter. "They will find me again anyway," he says. "But this time I will be ready for them."

Maria bursts into tears.

"Oh, I wish I could make love to you right now, sweet Nacho," Britney says as she starts to climb onto the bed.

"Come now Miss," says the doctor. "I need to examine that patient, check his vitals, and make sure he's on his way to recovery."

"Yes, of course," she says.

"Later baby," she tells Nacho as she blows him a kiss. "Right now I'm going to find the men who did this to you and...."

"Oh no," says Nacho.

"Britney, please," says Maria.

"Wait," says the doc.

Britney looks at each of them as she turns to go. "No one messes with my man and gets away with it," she growls.

# Chapter Fifteen

"You look absolutely ravishing today, Claudia," says Emilio as he escorts the young woman from El Rey del Frijol's corporate limo and into the deserted mining town of Las Lomas.

She gives him a perfunctory smile. The truth is she feels a little hypocritical arriving at the proposed home of her peasants army in such an expensive car, with such a well dressed man.

Of course, the desert wind has its way with the car and Emilio's fine clothing, and within minutes both are covered with a humbling layer of dust.

Claudia is much more familiar with the wind and its purpose, and so she stands proudly against the elements and shelters her eyes for a moment as she surveys the location.

Las Lomas, like so many abandoned mining towns, consists mostly of rows and rows of low, ramshackle, buildings: employee sleeping quarters and a few tiny single-family residences clustered together closer toward the town. There's an old cemetery with untended and overturned gravestones and, a short walk past the housing compound, a main street with a central store, a bar, a defunct gas station, and the mining headquarters building. The entire place is quite distant from the mines themselves.

The buildings look as though they've been sandblasted, which they have been... literally. The wood on the buildings looks almost new, their surface refreshed every time the wind blows and the swirling sand tears at the walls. Still, many of the buildings still have glass in their windows. And there's furniture as well: beds and tables and chairs. A few homes even have stoves with firewood still piled nearby them. Some kitchens are still stocked with dry goods and dishes stacked beside deep country sinks. Many bedrooms still have blankets on the beds and clothes in the closets. It's as though, when the mine closed, the workers took nothing with them, just abandoned what was there, and headed off to their next job in the cities or back to their homes in the smaller villages.

"This can be your headquarters, beautiful lady," says Emilio as he opens the door to the mining office. The area is big, with an entryway leading up to a large, polished wooden counter, beyond which are several old fashioned metal desks.

"Most importantly look up there," says Emilio and he points to a rather modern air conditioning unit mounted high on the office wall.

"The mine bosses knew how to live," adds Antonio. "I like it. A proper office for a heroic leader."

Claudia rolls her eyes. "I'm no one's hero," she murmurs.

"Oh, but you are," answers Emilio. "Haven't you seen the morning newspaper?"

"From where, sir," asks Claudia.

"From your home town of Chubasco, from Tijuana, even from Mexico City, and everywhere in between."

He opens a newspaper that he has been carrying folded under his arm. He holds it in front of Claudia so that she can read the headline and see the image a reporter took in the village square that day after church.

'MEXICAN HEROINE VOWS TO STOP DRIVEL'S WALL"

Claudia's image is spectacular even in the muddied half-tone print of the Chubasco paper. Her fist is raised into the air; her expression is full of resolve. Her beauty, Emilio knows, is undeniable.

"You could be a movie star if you wanted to be," whispers Antonio as he moves up beside Claudia.

"It's not something I ever even thought of," she answers.

"Hey, it would get you into the north." Antonio leans on the counter and smiles at her. "You know, make a few films, earn a few million, come back and buy all the land along the border so Drivel *can't* build his wall."

Claudia giggles. "Thanks for keeping me grounded," she whispers.

Antonio snatches the newspaper from Emilio and presses it toward the girl. "Can I have your autograph, Miss?"

Claudia giggles again and pretends to sign it with a flourish.


Emilio doesn't like it, doesn't like the closeness of the young man and woman, doesn't like the idea that he communicates with her so easily and she likes him so much.

"Stop the nonsense," Emilio grumbles. "I have someone I want you to meet, Señorita." And he leads them past the front office desks into a large paneled room that must have been the headquarters of the manager of the mine. The bespectacled woman who recorded Claudia's fiery speech sits behind the desk pounding away at her laptop computer. She still wears her jeans and her red sweater.

"Ah good, you're here," she says as she shuts the laptop, pushes her glasses up onto the bridge of her nose and gets to her feet.

97

"Rosie Alvarez," she says as she holds out her hand to Claudia.

"I'm Claudia..."

"I know who you are," answers Rosie. "I'm a big fan, a *really* big fan. "And this is Antonio," she continues as she turns to him, "anyone ever call you Tony?"

"Usually not," answers Antonio.

"Okay good, then I won't either."

"Now, Claudia, I'd like to take some pictures of you and Don Juan."

The young woman looks confused for the first time that day. "Do I know him?" she asks. "Do we know someone named Don Juan, Antonio?"

"The guy from the opera or the play or whatever it is?" asks Antonio.

Rosie turns toward Emilio and so do Claudia and Antonio.

"He's one of our security men, ex-military," says Emilio, "a great guy, former commander in the Mexican Army, actually. He's here to help whip your troops into shape."

Claudia sighs and shakes her head. "I don't have any troops," she says. "Not yet anyway."

"Of course you have troops beautiful lady," Emilio answers. And he walks to a door at the back of the office and opens it. There, standing across the dusty street are several dozen young men and women in rough workers clothes.

"They've come here to fight beside you," says Rosie.

"Odd," says Antonio, "They're looking away from us."

"Yes, what are they looking at?" asks Emilio.

"Oh, that," answers Rosie. "The Virgin in the tree."

"There's a virgin up in that tree?" asks Antonio.

Rosie giggles, "There may be," she says, "But the crowd is looking at the image of the Virgin of Guadalupe."

"What happened," says a very masculine voice that Claudia and Antonio have never heard before, "is that someone came to see you the other day, Claudia, and while she was here, she said that she saw the image of the Virgin Mary in the bark of that big tree across the way."

Claudia turns to see a very tall, handsome man in his middle 40s. He's clean-shaven and dressed in military fatigues.

"Don Juan?" she asks.

"Pleased to meet you, Claudia."

She offers him her hand, and he kisses it. Antonio starts to move forward and Don Juan turns and offers his hand to him.

Antonio adjusts his momentum rather quickly and well, Rosie thinks, as he accepts the handshake and smiles.

"Our new trainer?" Antonio asks.

"I prefer the American term," Don Juan answers... "Military advisor."

Antonio grimaces. He remembers his history books and how the term was used during the Viet Nam war... for soldiers who were gradually drawn into a bloody military conflict that seemed endless.

# Chapter Sixteen

President of the United States, Daniel Drivel, sits at his desk in the oval office. He wears his usual outfit: red business suit, white shirt, red tie, red shoes, and white socks. If he were a little jollier, he might look like Santa Claus. But he's not.

He's playing with action figures. In his right hand, he holds a toy version of himself: long blond hair, pot belly, slouched posture, but dressed as the comic book superhero, Captain USA.

"DAH DUM!" He croaks, as up over the edge of the desk, he raises the action figure of Pancho Villa: sombrero, long drooping mustache, and gun belts crisscrossing his chest.

"I will murder your women and children and rape your dogs and your cats," says Drivel pretending to be Pancho. His Mexican accent is terrible: high, squeaky, and insulting, but he's enjoying it as he raises Villa's gun-toting arm and charges the American action figure.

"Not on my watch, hombre," the president shouts in a much lower, more heroic voice as he stands, and smashes both action figures together, concentrating on the combat intently.

"I will never surrender, Señor!"

"Then you will die because I am the leader of the free world; I am the President of the United States. The people elected me, all of them. I got ALL of the popular votes every last one except for those pinkos in California!"

"I don't believe you," answers Drivel in his whiny Pancho Villa voice.

"Then you are an agent of the lying, liberal media who just want to give away this country to the filthy poor."

The toy conflict becomes more and more intense; finally, Captain USA rams his shield into the Villa figure, and Pancho flies across the room landing unceremoniously in a potted palm.

Drivel raises the American action figure in front of his eyes and smiles. "I knew we could count on you, Captain. You're just what we need to make American great again."

Suddenly there's a smattering of applause. Drivel sticks out his lips in an ugly pout. He looks up and sees a thin, well-dressed young man standing by the door observing him.

"I won, Gerald, did you see it?"

"Yes, Mr. President, I did."

"Good, you're a good boy, Gerald. And I have your undying loyalty, right?"

"Of course, sir."

"Wonderful. Now, what can you do for me?"

The young man carries a thick report to the president's desk and places it carefully in the center. Drivel sits, flips open the report, shudders, and eyes Gerald angrily.

"This is more than one page! You know I don't read reports that are more than one page."

"But it's important, Mr. President. It's about homeland security."

"And you know I don't like the Department of Homeland Security. I don't even meet with those bastards. Someone goes to the meetings for me and brings back a complete summary... in less than one page. So, why do I even have this thing?"

"It has to do with Mexico and the wall, Mr. President. Something is going on down there."

"It doesn't matter what's going on. I'm going to build that wall. It will be a great wall... a big, beautiful, gorgeous wall... especially from the American side, I don't care what it looks like from the Mexican side, but Mexico is going to pay for it anyway, and they are going to love doing it."

"I'm just saying that there's activity in Mexico near the area where we plan to build the newest section of the wall."

"Okay... okay. But I don't want to look at this piece-of-shit report. Just tell me what it says."

Gerald nods, takes a step forward, and begins.

"Activity near the site of the newest stretch of wall suggests that the Mexicans are planning some kind of invasion."

"An invasion? You're kidding me."

"No sir."

Do I have a hotel down there, a tower, a casino, a park, even a Laundromat?"

"Mr. President, listen. There are indications that the Mexicans are planning to invade the United States with a small army."

"An army is planning an invasion near one of my hotels. Is it on the American side or the Mexican side?"

"Sir, you do have shares in a small casino operating near San Antonio."

"Okay, call general Cox and have this invasion suppressed right away... Cox is still in command, isn't he? If not, call one of my other generals."

"Mr. President, don't you think we should find out more about what's going on before we just go down there and invade?"

"Gerald, I love to invade. It's one of the things I do best. I'm the president. Remember that fantastic bombardment of Somalia?"

"Yes, sir, though I'd like to forget it."

"Well, I'm not going to wait around like those former presidents, Eisenhower and Carter and Kennedy and all the rest of them. I'm a man of action. I've already told you what Mexicans are really like, right?"

"Yes, Mr. President," Gerald shudders at his memory of the president's vicious words. Then he turns serious again. "But sir, do you want intel or not?"

"Look, I'm packing up to play golf. Go down to the border yourself and find out about this new Mexican army."

"I'm happy to, of course, sir. But why don't we send someone from the intelligence community, an experienced member of the CIA who could work her way into the inner circles of Mexican power?"

"I don't like anyone in the intelligence community. They're all against me. They keep creating fake intel. The press is against me too. They keep making up fake news. So, just get me a report as soon as possible. Send someone else if you need to; just make it someone I can trust."

"Sir, we have an agent down there... a woman, and you even know her. She was a contestant in the Miss Universe pageant."

"Is she beautiful?"

"Of course sir, her name is Appassionata Sanchez."

"Oh, yes, I do remember her. She squealed when she met me. It was exhilarating. I had her named Miss Congeniality."

"Excellent, sir."

"Okay, send Appassionata to me first so I can interview her, check her out again, see how loudly she'll squeal this time. If she's a good girl, we can send her to Mexico."

"Thank you, Mr. President," says Gerald.

"De nada," answers Daniel Drivel.

# Chapter Seventeen

Clayton Bailey lifts the saddle from a rack in his spacious man cave and throws it over a life-sized plastic replica of a horse.

"Whoa, Silverado," he croons patting the critter's painted flank. "Steady big fella."

He flips up the stirrup and tightens the cinch around old Silverado. "Steady now... good boy."

Then he turns to a gun rack spread out below a mammoth movie poster. Bailey gazes for a moment into the deep eyes of one of his heroes, Randolph Scott.

"Ride The High Country," mumbles Bailey "that's what I gotta do tonight." Then he strides over to the rack, grabs his favorite pair of pearl-handled six-shooters, jams them into his holster, and is on his way back to good-old plastic Silverado when he hears a loud knock on the front door of his rambling ranch-style home.

"Answer that," he shouts, and soon he hears the familiar shuffle of Andy Meyer's boots as they head toward the entryway.

The door opens. He hears a high-pitched female voice, Britney's voice. His girl has come to pay him a visit he thinks. YE HAH! But she sounds angry. Meyers sounds a little angry himself. He starts shouting something, but whatever it is it doesn't stop Britney from marching her pink cowgirl boots toward Bailey's den. Within a few seconds the door flies open and the signing cowgirl marches in, pistol drawn.

"What is it, babe," he asks with a sheepish grin.

"You big prick!" she shouts.

"Well, actually you always complained that...."

SHUT UP!" she shouts. Britney turns and looks behind her for a moment, then motions with her pistol. "You two! Get in here and up against that RED RIVER poster."

Meyers and a badly shaken Toronto scuttle over against the far wall where the poster hangs.

"You too, dip shit," she says.

"But, baby...." Bailey moans.

"OVER AGAINST THE WALL!"

"What is it Brit, you seem upset," says Bailey as he heads over next to his friends.

"As if you didn't know," growls the cowgirl.

"No. Actually..."

A shot rings out and a bullet pulverizes the floor right in front of Bailey.

"Hey, wait," he moans, "that's hard wood," and he reaches into his back pocket and pulls out his mask.

"You don't want to mess with the masked man, little lady."

Britney answers him with another shot into the floor, this one decidedly closer. All three men pull back even more tightly against the wall.

"Now listen Brit," says Meyers.

The singing cowgirl turns and plugs him right in the shoulder. "Shut up big guy. I didn't come here to kill you."

"You mean," Bailey says as he suddenly begins to tremble.

"That's right, masked asshole, I'm here to end your miserable life."

Bailey throws his hands up in the air, "But *why* darlin'?"

"Do the words 'I LOVE NACHO' mean anything to you?"

"Not that piece of Mexican shit...."

"Uncle Clayton," whispers Toronto. "Meyer's here is hurt pretty bad, eh. Better make friends with the girl."

"Ka-BLAM!" Britney wizzes a shot right by the kid's temple.

"Oh Jesus," he moans as he trembles and slides onto the floor. Meyers slides down right beside him, and they both lie there moaning.

Britney turns to the two men. "Sorry guys," she sighs, and Bailey takes the opportunity to pull out his six-shooter and point it at her.

"Okay, babe, drop the gun."

"Uh-uh," says Britney. "You know I can outshoot you, Clayton."

"Not this time around," says Bailey and he slowly begins to move toward the door.

"Sorry about the collateral damage, but I came here to kill you, and that's what I intend to do."

"Don't think so," says Bailey, and he pulls the trigger.

The bullet ricochets off the overhanging metal lights and back toward Meyers hitting him directly in the other shoulder.

"Jeez," curses Toronto. "Can't we get a break here?"

Bailey shoots again and this time the bullet embeds itself into the poster right behind Britney. He's nailed Randolph Scott right between the eyes.

Britney bites her lip and shoots. The bullet strikes Bailey's pistol and it flies out of his hand. The gun flips up into the air and Britney catches it. But in the split second that her attention is diverted Bailey slips out of the door and closes it behind him.

Britney turns to Meyers and Toronto. "Sorry Mr. Meyers," she says. "Didn't come here to shoot you. But I've got to get that bastard."

"I understand," says Toronto. "But you can call 911, before you go, eh?"

"Are you pressing charges against me?" asks the girl.

"No, that's okay," moans Meyers. "Just call 911, and then let us get the hell out of here."

"You know where *I'm* goin', eh?" asks Toronto.

"Back to Canada?"

"You bet."

"And I'm going to Ecuador," adds Meyers. "Best climate in the world. Anyway, we don't plan to stick around and prosecute you, Ms. Britney."

"That's awful nice," says the singing cowgirl. She pulls out her phone and orders an ambulance for her victim. Then she walks up slowly and kisses each of them on the cheek.

"Bye," she coos, but then her eyes turn steely, as she turns and heads out the door in pursuit of The Lone Stranger.

# Chapter Eighteen

"I feel like I'm chaperoning two young lovers," says Padre Carlos.

"Why so?" asks Commander Don Juan Rodriquez.

Padre Carlos smiles. "Because in the old days, old aunts, grandmothers, or sometimes even a priest would walk several paces behind a couple as they courted... you know, to make sure there was no freshness."

"No hanky-panky," adds Tío Rafael as he smiles with memories of how he and the once-sweet Tía Lucinda dodged the chaperones and made love in the moonlight.

Up ahead though, Claudia and Antonio are deadly serious. "Do you think the gringos will really believe that we intend to launch an invasion from here?"

Now, Don Juan jogs up to them. He's heard what Antonio said, and he responds.

"They don't really respect our military prowess. So they probably figure it's just another example of what they perceive as Mexican incompetence."

"If we were to plan a real invasion where should it come from," asks Claudia.

Don Juan squints, looks around, and gets a certain glint in his eyes that he's probably stolen from some movie actor, Johnny Depp, perhaps. "I'd say, Juarez, much closer to a major metropolitan area, access that can be better protected. Even if they expect the attack, it may succeed. Large parts of it would be urban warfare."

Rafael and the priest have overtaken Claudia and the men by now.

"You asked about an invasion of the United States?" asks Tío Rafael.

"Actually I didn't," says the Commander.

"Ah, but if you had, I could tell you stories, son, about what it was like to participate in the real Mexican invasion of North America."

The old man now jerks his pistol out and waves it around dangerously until Padre Carlos grabs the gun, pulls it away from Rafael, and hands it to Claudia.

She smiles and tucks it into her belt.

"Ah, those were golden days," Rafael continues without his pistol. "I rode with Pancho Villa you know, and we DID invade the US and fought The Battle of Columbus. I killed nearly a hundred gringos myself. What a fighter! I was there, the bravest of them all. Magnificent!"

The Commander shrugs. "Did you see General Black Jack Pershing?"

"Oh, he chased us, young man, I can tell you that, throughout Northern Mexico, but he never came close to catching us and, once we drove him away, he never returned."

"Uh, I'm not sure you repelled him, sir," says Don Juan. "I think the outbreak of World War One prevented his return to the border."

"Think what you'd like, boy," Rafael, answers. "Pancho and I and our men, DID invade the United States, we did not *pretend* to invade."

Claudia smiles indulgently at her Uncle. She's again about to remind him that if he rode with Pancho in the battle of

Columbus, he would be well over one hundred and ten years old by now. But she's too kind. Instead, she turns to the Commander and asks, "But what if we were only pretending to attack, Juan, where should our mock invasion come from?"

Don Juan studies her for a moment and then smiles. "If you want to PRETEND to attack, Mujer, then you should pack up your guns, go home, and play with your dolls. Now excuse us," he says as he takes Antonio by the arm and marches with him ahead of the others, "The *men* have to talk."

Claudia turns red with anger. "Pompous ass! Male chauvinist pig!" she curses.

"Maybe so, Claudia," says Padre Carlos. "But we need him and his ability to train our people. You can't fake the invasion of a country and expect to pull it off without some demonstrable knowledge of soldiering."

"You're absolutely right, father," says Antonio as he returns to them. He confronted Don Juan about his chauvinist attitude and the soldier has marched away.

"Listen," says Antonio. "We let that blowhard train whatever army we can put together, let it become a great distraction. The press will come. They'll report what they see. If we're realistic enough, we'll soon draw vigilantes, peace marchers, the cops, the army, the whole Rancho Grande."

"A peasant army is massing on the US Mexican border!" says Claudia gesturing as though she were reading from a banner plastered across the sky.

"We'll be protesting the stupidity of the wall they are building," adds Rafael. "We'll act like we are going to attack and take out a few crews of wall builders."

"YES," says Antonio.

"Then the real strike force enters the US secretly."

"As tourists," croaks Tío Rafael, "maybe on a bus."

"Right, right," adds Antonio, "We take a tour of the Alamo but when it's time to leave...."

Rafael suddenly jerks his pistol away from Claudia and begins waving it over his head again. "We seize the mission and hold it. Si se Puede."

"While Juan and his army march around here at the border and draw everyone's attention," adds the priest. "The US Army will be focusing on them. All the politicians will. All the press will be here."

"An interesting proposal," says Commander Don Juan as he returns to the others. "My apologies beautiful lady," he says to Claudia. "Sometimes we military men get so caught up in ourselves that we forget what talented fighters you women can be."

"Thank you Señor," she says, and she nods to Antonio as if to thank him too.

"Now," Don Juan Rodriquez begins, "this is what we do next...."

A hawk circles lazily above the group: an old man, a young man, a priest, a soldier and a dreamer. They are whispering now, even though they don't have to. This is in fact, the first real assembly of Claudia's Army–the group that fully intends to recapture the Alamo... if only for a moment.

*"Si Se Puede!"*

The cry rings across the deserts of Northern Mexico. But this time it is wild, bold, demanding! Shouted by the gravelly voice of Pancho Villa himself. (At least that's how Tío Rafael imagines it.) In his mind he sees Pancho drilling a band of almost five hundred strong men and women. They battle with swords and blast their guns at straw men made in the image of the gringo.

"Take over, Compadre," Pancho shouts to his right-hand man, Rafael Hector Salvador Madero.

111

"With Pleasure," answers the dashing Mexican, and he drives his magnificent white steed into the ranks of the trainees. He wields a sword and is so handsome, so competent that all the women warriors' hearts flutter madly. He is wise beyond his years, think the experienced soldiers, and of course, he is dreaming.

What Tío Rafael actually sees are men and women carrying pitchforks, rakes, and hoes, though a few do have rifles. There are teenagers and even some small boys among them. Don Juan, dressed in a stripped down version of his Mexican Army uniform, is running along beside them, shouting commands.

The rag-tag group of volunteers numbers at fewer than one hundred. But one hundred is not a bad number for starters, and the fifteen or so strong young men among the trainees will do well in battle, or at least in a fictional battle.


Ah, but the women are so powerful, imagines Claudia. In her mind she sees herself standing high on a hill overlooking her massing troops. She dresses like La Adelita, the valiant Mexican warrior woman. She wears bandoliers strapped across her chest, holds a pistol in her hand, and shouts fierce commands at her soldiers-in-training. In this imagining, Juan and Antonio are Commanders under her direction.

"This way," she gestures as she grabs a pitchfork and jabs it in the air as though attempting to skewer those gabachos. For a moment Claudia's eyes clear and she sees the reality. Among the volunteers there are only a handful of strong young women. There are also girls in their early teens and older women some nearly sixty who want to become part of the fight. It is Don Juan who trains them, and Claudia thinks, he is doing a good job, molding these volunteers into an army that will at least catch the attention of the press.

Antonio is not so sure. He thinks Don Juan doesn't know what he is doing as he and his men try to get one contingent or another to actually march. "Hold your ranks there," shouts Juan's fellow soldier-volunteer Hector Miranda, as a platoon of newcomers tries to learn how to stay in line.

And suddenly Antonio imagines himself leading the brigade as they step smartly across the desert. "Eyes right!" he calls as they pass a reviewing stand of political and military leaders.

"Isn't that even the President of the United States on the reviewing stand?" Antonio wonders in his imaginings. "And doesn't President Drivel have a very worried look on his face?"

"How are we doing?" asks Don Juan interrupting the excited dreams of his compadres.

Antonio snaps back to reality. He looks down at his dust-covered boots. This wasn't what he imagined, or what he had hoped for, even as a diversion from their attack on The Alamo.

"They're still not there." He whispers.

"Of course not, amigo," says Don Juan cheerfully. "Give us time, a few more men and women, some uniforms, and we will have a virtual army for you. They may not be able to fight, but they will give the appearance of a real force."

All four members of the group from Chubasco gather around Don Juan now, and suddenly he smiles at them.

"I see the visions in your eyes, my friends. And you can help me."

"I'd like that," murmurs Claudia.

"Good. Can you shoot a rifle?"

"Since I was a little girl and my father took me hunting in the mountains."

"Great, then you will help train shooters with the new rifles our benefactor has provided."

He turns and looks at the others.

"You must all help, amigos, for time is short."

113

They nod eagerly.

And soon, Antonio is bare-chested, leading the troops across a rough obstacle course that the soldier-volunteers have constructed. Rafael coaches the old men and women in fierce shouts and facial expression while they swing their farm tools like deadly weapons. Claudia leads the teenagers in target practice. Padre Carlos discusses maps and tactics with some of the prime recruits who just might be part of the Alamo incursion. Don Juan oversees all and, from his latest interactions with Antonio, it appears that the two are learning to get along.

# Chapter Nineteen

Far behind enemy lines, at the Faithful Chicken Bar back in Chubasco, in fact, Old Tío Rafael sits alone in a small booth in the back corner. Half a pitcher of icy margaritas sweats onto the tabletop in front of him. He's come home to gather a few more supplies. So, why not stop in for a drink. He can return to the border and Claudia's Army tomorrow.

Right now, he's very drunk, amusing himself by smashing a plateful of refried beans with his fork, sculpting it into a map of Northern Mexico and the Southwestern United States.

He takes his knife and carves a sharp line along the Rio Grande where the border should be.

"Mi Frontera," he mumbles as he reaches for a tortilla, tears it into small pieces and begins jabbing the chunks along the border as though they were columns of troops massing for an invasion.

"Magnífico," he calls as he lowers his chin onto the table and studies the formation from eye level.

Suddenly, a delicate feminine hand with brightly polished red fingernails reaches in and begins repositioning the tortilla troops.

"I'm afraid you are making some tactical errors, General," says a strong feminine voice. Rafael looks up and sees a fabulous Mexican woman in her early forties. She wears a high-buttoned, starched, white cotton blouse and a tight-fitting black skirt.

"Excuse me, Miss," responds Rafael, as he looks the woman up and down. "Exactly what are you doing?"

She smirks at him. "Why, helping you, of course, General. Tactically, that is. May I join you?"

Rafael is too stunned to say anything for a moment. Then he nods, and the woman reaches up, unpins her hair and shakes it free. Long, ebony locks swirl around her face. She wears dark red lipstick and heavy eye makeup. Her form is highly athletic and muscular. She also wears very high heels that let her tower over the old Mexican warrior.

"My name is Appassionata Sanchez," she says. "Are we planning an invasion?"

She flutters her lashes at him, smiles sweetly, cocks her head, and asks, "Care to share a margarita with me? Or are you saving them all for yourself?"

"Oh no, of course, not," says the old man as he jumps to his feet and reaches for the pitcher of margaritas, almost spilling it in the process. Still, he raises the pitcher. Appassionata grabs his wrist to steady him. Her touch is so firm that Rafael sighs and swallows hard.

Appassionata pulls a glass from the corner of the table, places it under the lip of the pitcher, and helps him pour some of the cooling liquid into it.

Rafael then lowers the pitcher and takes his seat.

"You have strong hands," she says.

The old man looks confused. He doesn't know what to say, and so he believes her.

"Well, yes. I rode with Pancho Villa, you know."

"That explains it. But you must have been so young then."

"Certainly."

Appassionata leans forward. "I'll bet you were a handsome bruit: dashing, charming. Am I not right, General?"

Tío Rafael nods.

"I'll bet all the women were in love with you."

A far away look fills the old man's eyes. He draws in a breath, comes as close to a swagger as he can and answers, "Well, of course. As I said, I rode with Pancho Villa. We spent many hours in consultation. And then there were the heroic battles...."

"Yes, yes."

"So there was very little time for the ladies, I'm afraid."

"But they admired you from afar," sighs Appassionata. "You broke many hearts without even knowing it."

Rafael laughs. "I suppose I did. The fortunes of war."

"And you are still very dashing, sir." The woman pours another margarita for Rafael. "May I say, you wear your years handsomely."

Rafael is turning bright red.

"And you are still a genuine bandido?"

The old man's brow furrows. "Not at all, I am a rebel and a freedom fighter."

Appassionata nods as she gestures to the plate full of beans and tortillas. "And these are the plans for your freedom fight?"

Rafael begins to feel a little nervous. He stares back at her. She winks, perhaps her one mistake.

For a moment the old man realizes that this beautiful woman is after more than his good looks and his companionship, and so he clears his throat, reaches for his hat, and begins to slide out of the booth. Appassionata reacts quickly.

"Señor Freedom Fighter..." she sighs, "Stay. The night is young, and we have so much to talk about."

She moves in closer, leans toward him and whispers, "I hear that rebels are making plans as we speak. Mexican Freedom Fighters intend a new invasion of the American South West.

"Do you know any of those freedom fighters, sir?" She slides her hand under the table and places it firmly on his thigh.

Rafael jumps. Her touch is electric. He gives her a crazy grin and begins to sweat. "I might."

Appassionata slides out of the booth, grabs a chair from a nearby table and swings it around so that the back is facing him. Then she straddles it. "I want you, general!"

Rafael swallows hard; his eyes bug out, and yet somehow he manages to whisper, "And I want you, Appassionata."

"But first we have business to do."

Rafael's hands are shaking; his mouth is half open. He tries to speak, but no words come out. Across the room, the bartender, the only other person in the cantina, stares, every bit as opened-mouthed and unbelieving as Rafael.

"Do you know where I can see a plan for the upcoming invasion?" the beautiful woman asks as she stands, pushes the chair away, strides proudly toward the old man and sits on his lap. She plants a deep kiss on his lips.

Rafael reels. He grabs her and kisses her back, and this time it is Appassionata who is thrilled. "Oh, my God," she sighs, "Who knew?"

Rafael smiles proudly, but suddenly he coughs, seems to be on the verge of a fatal heart attack. He gasps for breath; his eyes begin watering; he clutches his chest. Appassionata knows she must act quickly. "Show me!" she breathes into his ear.

"Yes!" he answers, and suddenly he jumps to his feet, almost knocking the beautiful woman to the floor in the process.

"I have the plans hanging in mi casa."

Appassionata brushes her hair back from her head dramatically. "Take me to them."

"It would be an honor."

And with that the couple strides from the cantina as the bartender watches them in disbelief.

#

Tía Lucinda is at the border with the other members of Claudia's Army helping to organize and manage the kitchen crew that is feeding the ever-growing numbers of troops. Meanwhile, the old ramshackle home she and Tío Rafael share seems to sleep in the evening's warmth. Until that is, the old man flips on the lights illuminating not only a well kept Mexican kitchen (no thanks to the old man) but a wide living room with a huge satellite map of the border pinned to the wall.

Apparently, Tío Rafael wasn't lying. The map shows the location of Claudia's Army as the troops stretch out along the Rio Grande. Far more damning, though is the yellow marker line that shows the secret invasion route as it snakes across the border and up toward San Antonio and the Alamo.

Fortunately, perhaps, Claudia's uncle never finished drawing the line. It ends somewhere outside of San Antonio near a strange rambling building that looks a little like the beloved shrine itself.

Appassionata strides up to the map, her hands on her hips. She grins.

"So it's all-true," she says. "Who would have believed it?"

"Anyone who realizes that I rode with Pancho Villa, of course," Rafael answers and for just a moment the spy doesn't know what to make of the comment.

"But the invasion is incomplete," Appassionata adds. "Exactly where are your troops headed, you handsome devil?"

Rafael doesn't want to seem incompetent; he doesn't want to admit that he never finished the map, or that he may not really be a handsome devil. He looks around the room desperately for some clue, some indication that will save his evening with the lovely woman.

"Why there. There!" he says at last pointing to the strange structure on the map.

"But what is it?" Appassionata asks as she moves even closer.

"It is what it is," answers Rafael with a sudden lucidity that he's almost never before possessed in his life, perhaps God's gift to those aged or insane, or maybe just something he learned from Pancho Villa.

But Appassionata seems to understand.

"YES!" she says, her eyes suddenly glowing. "I recognize it now. I've been there; it's that great restaurant... the one that they modeled on The Alamo... The Best Tacos in Texas... it's THE ALAMO TAQUERIA."

"Would you like some Tequila?" Rafael asks softly.

Appassionata nods. Then she pulls out her cell phone and snaps a few quick pictures of the wall map while the old man scurries to the cupboard to get a big bottle.

"How clever of you," she says. "Why try to seize a national shrine and arouse the public ire, when you can capture a replica, and – in banner headlines and photos across all the world's great newspapers – it will look like you captured the shrine? You'll make the same political statement without any of the risk.

"Given the right spin, this is far more effective."

"Now, about that Tequila?" Tío Rafael says holding up the bottle and two glasses.

"Thank you, no," the spy says coldly, and she turns abruptly and walks out the door.

Tío Rafael shrugs sadly. But then he smiles. "Oh well, more for me," he sighs and pours himself a drink.

Very soon after, however, details of the impending invasion reach Washington and Mexico City, and both Daniel Drivel and Ricardo de la Palma Alta, the President of Mexico, issue orders sending troops to the border as Appassionata Sanchez heads toward Washington to explain things further.

# Chapter Twenty

Penny Pringle, a pretty young nurse's aid in a candy-stripe dress and sensible shoes, rolls Nacho's wheel chair out of the hospital's front entrance and in between the long row of cars in the reserved parking area.

Nacho is finally well enough to go home, to be cared for by someone who loves him... and that someone is Britney Fleming... at least that's what *she* has decided.

The singing cowgirl stands beside her little pink jeep and opens the passenger side door. She smiles at Nacho eagerly.

"Where's Maria?" the big man asks.

"We don't need her, do we, babe," Britney answers. "I can take care of you all by myself."

Nacho frowns in confusion. "But where will I sleep? Maria at least has a separate room and...."

"Don't trouble yourself," Britney sighs as she walks up to Nacho and places a gentle kiss on his forehead. "I'll take care of everything. I'll get you back on your feet and then we can...."

Before the little blonde can say another word, the clip clop of horse's hooves rings across the parking lot.

Britney, Nacho, and Penny Pringle turn toward the sound and see Clayton Bailey dressed in his baby blue shirt and jeans, blue cowboy boots, his Stetson hat and that ridiculous mask, astride an enormous white horse. It's a live stallion this time, and it moves slowly past the cars and comes directly to Britney and Nacho.

"I should have finished you off the last time we met, fat man," growls Bailey. "But, hell... what's the difference? You die today, right now, right here in this blasted hospital parking lot."

Nacho looks up at the masked man. Bailey looks a hundred times bigger on top of the stallion. Still, Nacho smiles. "You wouldn't shoot an unarmed man, would you, cabron?"

Bailey snickers, "A-course I would." Then he turns to the nurse.

"Just roll his sorry ass out into the middle of the road for me, would you, pretty Miss? You know, so's I kin execute him, right proper."

Penny Pringle glances over at Britney who shakes her head.

"No way, Jose," answers Penny.

"Don't you dare call me one of those dirty Mex'kin names, bitch," Bailey answers. "I said, roll that som-bitch...."

And then Britney steps fully in front of Nacho, blocking him from Bailey and the guns she can see in his holsters.

She doesn't say a word, just turns to reveal a pearl handled pistol hanging low around her waist. She crouches forward, ready to draw.

"Do not forsake me oh my darlin'," whispers Nacho.

"Get out a' my way, girl," Bailey growls. "You can't save that sack a shit."

She sneers. "He's *my* sack a shit, and I'm gonna save him."

"You say that to almost every man you meet," Bailey counters, "But you can't help this hombre. I'm going to fill him full a lead."

"Not a chance, cowboy."

Britney begins moving slowly around to the left, her arms held away from her body, just above her guns. Her fingers twitch like some western movie gunslinger. Bailey and his horse turn with her until they're no longer facing Nacho. They're standing at the head of the long roadway through the parking lot.

"I used to love you, you know," he croons. "But you've been corrupted Baby... drunk too much tequila, eaten too many fucking refried beans... kissed too many crazy Mex'kins, lost your mind. You're starting to think those people are just like the rest of us." He sighs sadly. "I'm afraid it's time I put you out of your misery."

Britney draws and fires so quickly that Penny doesn't even see the movement of her gun. She just sees Bailey's hat fly off of his head with a big bullet hole through the front of it.

The masked man gasps, looks at his hat laying on the ground behind him, sees the hole, and seems to wilt right there.

"Now, why'd you go and do that, Britney?" he whines. "That was my favorite hat."

The singing cowgirl doesn't answer. She just takes two big steps backwards and continues to glower at Bailey, daring the masked-man to draw on her.

"You're serious?" he asks.

"I was never more serious in my life, Lone Stranger. Now, get off the damn horse and face me like a man."

Bailey glances over at Nacho, "See the trouble you've caused, scumbag? I have to kill the love of my life just because she wants to save your sorry ass."

"Hey Bud!" Britney calls angrily to Bailey. "His ass ain't sorry. In fact, I've grown very fond of it."

"Your bottom is pretty wonderful too, Britney," Nacho coos lovingly.

"JUST SHUT THE 'F' UP WILL YOU," Bailey shouts. And he swings his leg over his horse and jumps down onto the pavement.

"All right then," he says as he assumes the same posture as the girl: the challenging, hands-by-your-guns, forward leaning, jaw-locked' pose from High Noon and countless other westerns.

"Draw, sucker," hisses the cowgirl.

"Lady's first," answers Bailey. But, as he says it, he draws anyway... quickly... but not quickly enough. Britney shoots the gun out of his hand before he can get it fully in front of him. Then she returns her pistol to her holster before Bailey realizes what she's done.

"That's some fancy shootin', babe," says Nacho.

A smile touches Britney's lips, but she doesn't loose her concentration, just deftly shoots Bailey's second gun out of his hand when he tries to fake her out with another quick draw. The gun flies high in the air and lands across from him.

"Damn, woman! You destroyed my favorite pistol," Bailey moans. Only then does he realize that the girl still has her gun drawn, and he is unarmed.

"This is *my* man," she hisses nodding toward Nacho. "And you'd better leave him alone. Do you understand?"

"Yes ma'am," answers Bailey.

"Now dance, sidewinder!" And she begins to pepper the ground around Bailey's feet with shots that have him skipping and jumping to avoid loosing a toe or even a foot. But soon the singing cowgirl has emptied her gun and fired several blank shots. She looks at her revolver for just a moment, and that's when the masked man pulls a tiny pistol from behind his back and starts to aim, when suddenly:

Ka-BLAM!

A loaded water bottle slams off the side of Bailey's head, tearing a gash in his cheek, and making his shot go wild.

Britney pulls her own tiny pistol from behind her back and plugs Bailey right in the shoulder.

Then she turns to Nacho. "You saved me babe."

Nacho nods. "Not an easy throw when you're all bandaged up," he says.

Bailey lies on the ground moaning and sobbing, bleeding too badly to get to his feet.

Britney strides proudly over to Nacho, grabs him by his shirt, pulls him to her and kisses him passionately.

"Whoa," gasps the big man as he enjoys the kiss and more than a few casual gropes from his girlfriend. "Shooting someone turns you on?"

"Always has, big guy," she answers. "Always has."

Then she turns to Penny Pringle. "Get that piece of shit Bailey inside. See if they can fix up that shoulder of his."

"Yes, Ma'am," Penny answers, totally in awe of the cowgirl's prowess as a shooter.

"Only don't fix him up too quickly, know what I mean? Take your time."

And Penny Pringle nods knowingly.

# Chapter Twenty-One

A cactus wren darts out of a giant saguaro and flits upward into the glow of the Mexican sun. The bird circles, seizes a tiny insect out of the air, and darts back to her thorny home. She stands for a moment on the needles of the cactus and then hops back inside.

Claudia walks along the edge of the wall that divides her country from the United States. She watches the bird and wonders if the little wren knows that, like so many Mexican illegals, she just crossed the border in her pursuit of food for her children.

"Maybe the next bright idea from the American president," Claudia thinks, "will be to put up sky-high netting that will help keep Mexican birds out of the United States."

Claudia continues her walk. The border wall feels as though it's a mile high and impossible to breach. She stops to look up at the top of the barrier, and suddenly, it starts to rain, dampening her thoughts, but cooling her immediately.

Claudia turns her head skyward to catch a mouthful of rainwater and can't believe her eyes. That same blue, shimmering, watery triangle that she had first seen when she and Tío Joaquín tried to cross into America so many weeks ago is there again. It floats high above the wall dropping a curtain of rain along the monstrous barrier. Claudia does remember reading something about the phenomenon after her first encounter with it in the desert. What is it called? She asks herself. Oh yes, ATP, Atmospheric Triangular Phenomena.

Some religious leaders, she read, call it God's Tears, which are being shed over the current condition of humanity and the fact that people are treating each other and the planet so horribly. Scientists simply say that it's currently under investigation.

In any case, she wipes her eyes; she's drenched.

Of course, she'll be dry in a few minutes, but she's shivering now, wishing she could get out of these wet clothes. And then she spots a little shack a few yards away... an outpost of the old mining town that they have chosen for their military exercises. The building is not much more than a one room shack, but it was once a miner's home, and she knows there's a cot in there, maybe even a sheet or some blankets, a place to get out of her wet clothes and let them dry.


Inside the shack, it's shady and not as hot as she would have expected. Claudia strips out of her blouse and skirt and lays them on the ledge of the window to dry in the sun. She wraps herself in one of the light cotton sheets from the cot and lies down for a moment. She closes her eyes, not realizing how tired she is from all her effort. The preparation and training and exercise have taken their toll, and she falls asleep immediately.


Claudia dreams. She finds herself alone in the desert, walking through tumultuous winds that thrash her with sand and tear at her clothing.

Now, violently, angrily the desert ground swells, shudders and – suddenly – an endless, thick, black wall wrenches itself out of the earth and thrusts upward. When fully extended, perhaps a mile or more into the heavens, the massive structure stands there, looming over her threateningly.

It begins to tremble, to shudder and weave. For a moment it almost seems to lean down toward Claudia and scream warnings at her, and then suddenly jerks back upward.

The young woman cowers in its presence for a long moment, and then she smiles with determination and strides toward the imposing structure.

Claudia places her hand hard against the steel surface, which, even in the scorching desert heat, is cold to the touch.

"FALL YOU MONSTROSITY!" she screams. And the wall pulls back from her, trembles for a moment, shudders, and then the cold steel splits apart. Mile high girders totter in the boiling sun and then topple like falling redwood trees all around her.

A giant fissure opens all along the length of the wall and swallows up the rubble. Then, once again the ground shudders wildly and closes. The wind picks up blasting sand once again over everything... leaving nothing but a vast desert plain as though the wall had never been there at all.

"We can do this," Claudia whispers in her dream. And then she's nearly tossed from her cot as she's awakened by the same kind of rumbling sounds that she dreamed of.

She gets to her feet as the horrible chugging and whirring and pounding continue. She rushes to the window. The wall is still there, not shaken, not fallen. But the rumbling is still there too.

Claudia slips quickly into her clothes, moves to the doorway, and steps outside as a massive tank screams its way up to the shack. A teenager in goggles and a skullcap sits looking out of the top turret. He's sporting a crazy grin. Claudia rushes toward him. She jumps up onto the vehicle, climbs to the turret and stands there yelling, "STOP! STOP!"

The tank stops.

"What the hell is this?" Claudia asks the kid.

"Hector Oliva, at your service," he answers.

"Who?"

"Hector Oliva?"

Claudia studies the young man recognizing the name and even some of his distinct features.

"You're related to THE Hector Oliva?"

"Yeah, he's my dad."

"El Rey del Frijol, The King of Beans?"

"Yeah, and we both support your cause. Course, the tank was my idea. I figured you could use it here at the border. So, should I start by knocking down this section of the wall?"

"NO!" Claudia says.

"Come on, why not?"

"Just drive back to our headquarters so we can talk this over?"

"Hey, if I ram that wall right now, I'll have the element of surprise."

"Yes *you* will, but then *we* will lose it. Think of the big picture, Hector."

"Junior. Call me Hector Junior."

"Okay, Hector Junior, please drive me back to camp, and we can tell you exactly how you can help us."

The kid pouts. "I need to ram that wall."

"No."

Hector Junior hangs his head like a spoiled little boy, which, of course, he is.

"Okay... I guess."

And then he pounds his fist hard against the tank and a panel slides open to reveal a snaggle toothed, bald headed tank driver.

"Sancho?" says the kid.

"Si?" answers Sancho.

"Back to the base, bro."

"We can't ram the wall?"

"Sorry, but NO."

"But I want to mow the damn thing down."

"Me too."

"Absolutely not," says Claudia.

"Okay, okay. Damn!" Then turning to Sancho he adds, "La mujer simplemente ne entiede la guerra."

Claudia's sighs. "Entinedo perfectamente, niño! Now get us back to headquarters."

"Yes, Ma'am."

Moments later the tank rumbles back into the heart of Los Lomas, the headquarters of Claudia's Army, with the young woman riding on the front. Hector Junior still sits in the turret though he's not as excited as he was a few minutes earlier.

Antonio, Don Juan, and Padre Carlos stand in the center of the street as the massive war machine comes to a stop in front of them.

"How did you stop him, Claudia?" Antonio asks. "We couldn't do it."

She just smiles.

"Impressive," says Don Juan. "Now get down here, kid, we need to talk."

Hector Junior scrambles out of the tank's hatch and jumps to the ground beside Claudia. As he does his driver slides open his little viewing window.

Hector salutes Don Juan who is the only person wearing any kind of military uniform. "At your service, General. I am

Hector Oliva Junior, The Prince Of Beans, and this is my driver, Sancho."

"Reporting for duty, comandante," adds Sancho.

Don Juan returns the salute and smiles. "So tell me, gentlemen, how did you obtain this tank?"

"You don't like it?" asks Hector Junior.

"Actually I do. It appears to be the latest model. Russian isn't it?"

"Got it from my Dad's fleet."

"Your father has a fleet of tanks?" asks Antonio.

"Just six."

Claudia shrugs. "Well, I guess he IS The King."

"At least of beans," adds Padre Carlos.

# Chapter Twenty-Two

Well-manicured fingers reach into a humidor and take out a fine Cuban cigar. They move it before the face of an enormously fat man who studies the cigar for a moment, sniffs it, and smiles anticipating the pleasure of smoking.

"Well, what are you waiting for, Miguel?" he growls suddenly. "Snip it off!" And an immaculately dressed young man takes a cutter from inside the box, brings it to the tip of the cigar, and cuts the end off neatly.

The fat man laughs. "You may be a little too good at that."

Miguel grins. "Better be careful, boss. You wouldn't want me sniping at you, now, would you?"

The fat man shrugs. "I think you know better than that."

"I do," Miguel answers as he strikes a match and moves it to the tip of the cigar. The fat man slips the cigar between his lips, and draws in the smoke.

He is Hector Oliva Senior... or, as Claudia and the rest of the world knows him, El Rey del Frijol, The King of Beans.

In spite of his bulk, he is dressed impeccably in a white linen suit, and he smiles at Miguel who shakes out the match and steps back.

"Thank you," says the King, "that will be all."

He watches as Miguel nods to him, turns, and marches from the room.

Emilio sits in front of the King's desk and watches too. "Impressive boy," he says.

"Yes," says the King, "More impressive than some members of my own family, I think."

Emilio flinches as though he's been punched.

"So, you are Antonio," the King says to the man Emilio has brought with him to the meeting.

"Yes sir."

"And I suppose you're wondering why I listen to my worthless brother when he gives me advice?"

"Actually no," says Antonio. "I don't know anything about your family or your relationship."

"Of course, of course," says the King as he gestures broadly with his cigar. "Forgive me. I thought everyone in Mexico knew about Emilio. He talks a good game, loves acting like the big shot, you know, going around scaring everyone. Usually there's a beautiful woman involved in these hair-brained schemes he comes up with."

Emilio starts to protest but the King just holds up his hand and he falls silent.

"In your case," the King tells Antonio, "I decided he might be right. This Claudia of yours..."

"She's not *my* Claudia, sir."

"No she's not, and that may just be the point. She's no one's Claudia but her own. She's a dreamer, a visionary, a Joan of Arc. Do you know how rare such people are? There are no more than a handful in every century."

"Then why isn't she here meeting with us?" asks Antonio. "I hate having meetings behind her back."

The King rises from his desk and moves around in front of it. He leans back against it, as Emilio knows that he does a dozen of times everyday when he wants to talk seriously.

"Because," says the King taking a long draw on his cigar, "She is pure and unspoiled."

"A beautiful dreamer, yes," adds Emilio.

"We need to keep her pure, Mr. Cervantes," says the King. "We need to keep her vision unsullied. Let her continue to look at the stars and inspire her followers. But *practical* people know that purity is just an illusion. Don't we, Antonio?"

"I'm not sure."

The King of Beans steps forward so that he's almost toe-to-toe with the young man. "Surely you must realize that pure patriotism, pure anything really, is a dream. It can work, but only if backed by people with other skills... *practical* skills. Someone has to be in the background doing the dirty work... the profitable work."

"And those people are?" asks Antonio.

"Who do you think, boy?" says the King.

"Are you saying that you didn't just provide the location and the weapons and the military advisors because you love Mexico and believe in Claudia?"

"Of course I love Mexico," answers The King of Beans. "But I'm a practical man and I recognize that your girl has a talent that is almost impossible to buy."

He pauses, studies his cigar and then glowers back at the two men in front of him.

"TRUST, gentlemen. You can't buy trust. The people trust her because she is so pure. She's come to believe so strongly in her dreams and her mission that we don't want to confuse her with practical considerations. We don't want to raise the idea that all things have a cost and someone somewhere has to pay the price. Leave her alone. Let her dream, let her inspire, let her succeed."

"But what do you want from her?" asks Antonio.

"If she does get what she wants... and that's not a given, but if she does, she will draw other powerful people to her."

"Like a magnet," adds Emilio.

"We want her connections to be ours. That's all."

"I'm not sure I understand," says Antonio.

"Nothing that will harm you or your beautiful Claudia... just introductions and associations."

"She need not even know that it's happening," says Emilio.

"But someone has to know... someone on her team," adds the King.

"And that would be me," says Antonio.

"Precisely."

Antonio stares at the King of Beans for a long moment, and then his face turns resolute.

"Precisely *not*," he says as he gets to his feet. "I'm sorry, gentlemen, but I know that Claudia would not be interested in your proposition. And I'm not either. I had hoped that your love of your country and its people motivated your desire to help us."

"But it does," says Emilio. His voice suddenly sounds almost desperate.

"I guess we'll find that out, won't we?" says Antonio, and he turns and walks from the room.

Emilio stares nervously at the door that has just closed behind the young man. He's afraid to turn and face his brother again, afraid of the consequences of this latest broken deal that he's tried so hard to arrange.

And then he jumps.

Loud, strong, almost godlike laughter startles him.

Emilio turns to his brother who is now right beside him, laughing so hard that he can barely stand up.

The King of Beans move up to Emilio and places his hand on his shoulder. He is still shaking with laughter.

"I can't believe it," says The King.

Emilio tries to pull away but can't. His brother's grip is too tight. Then The King's other hand comes to rest on Emilio's face, cradles it for a moment.

"It's amazing," Hector says. "For the first time in your life, brother, you have actually convinced me to do the right thing."

"Thank you, Emilio," says the King of Beans. And he pulls his brother to him and kisses him on the cheek.

# Chapter Twenty-Three

Claudia looks out the window at the yellow, blue, and pink crazy quilt sunset thrown across the sky.

"Lovely," she murmurs and then turns to look at the man with whom she shares the bedroom above her command headquarters.

"Handsome hombre," she sighs. "Tell me, Antonio, where did you get those broad shoulders and powerful arms?"

He looks up from a table full of lists, and he smiles. "My father," he answers, "And the Gulf of Mexico."

"Really?"

"The members of my family were fishermen you know, in the port of Tampico. And fishing means boats and boats mean swimming, and swimming and fishing means, you know... muscles."

He looks down at his half-naked body; the bedroom isn't the only thing he shares with his girl. Right now, he wears the pajama bottoms and she the tops. She's moving slowly toward him.

"And where," he asks, "Did you get those sexy... dimples?"

Claudia smiles, showing him just how cute they are.

"That's easy sir. From Nacho."

Antonio frowns. "Nacho? Another man? Should I be worried?"

She pads up to him on her little slippers. "I don't think so, mi amor. He taught everyone in our village to smile."

"And now he's picking melons with your sister, across the border."

Claudia moves behind Antonio, wraps her arms around him, and looks over his shoulder at the list he's making.

"Have you figured it out?"

"Members of our little strike force? I'm thinking Tomas and Micho, strong guys who know how to handle weapons and will be good in a fight."

"Do they know how to take orders, too?"

Antonio smiles. "Yes, general... always thinking of the chain of command, huh?"

"Someone has to."

"So, then we should add Padre Carlos?"

"He understands authority."

"Si, but not Tío Rafael."

"We should leave him behind to keep an eye on Don Juan and the kid with the tank."

Antonio flinches for a moment remembering his meeting with the kid's father.

"Worried about something?" Claudia asks.

"Yeah, how much longer I have to wait to kiss you," Antonio lies, then he feels better when he sees Claudia's eager smile in response. He pulls her to him and kisses her. The kiss is long and loving. She sighs, suddenly becoming the dreamer again. "This is all so thrilling."

"My kisses? You have no idea how many women in Tampico have said the very thing."

"I meant the adventure."

"Ah," Antonio pauses thoughtfully. "Then why not bring your sister?"

Claudia looks at him in surprise.

"Really, and Nacho?"

Antonio nods.

"That's a crazy idea."

"I don't know, why not share your greatest adventure with your best friend: your sister... and the kid who taught your whole village to smile."

Claudia looks at Antonio lovingly. He understands so much, she thinks.

"Good idea," she says. "Ka-BLAM!"

"What?"

"When you meet Nacho you'll find out what I mean."

"So then, call Maria."

"Right now?"

"That's an order, general."

Claudia glides across the bedroom and picks up her cell phone.

"Hey sis," Claudia sings into the phone. "¿Qué pasa?"

From no more than a hundred miles (but political light years) away comes the excited answer. "Claudia? What are you doing calling me this late at night?"

"Just wanted to check in. And I have something important to tell you."

"NO! Are you pregnant?" Maria asks jokingly.

"Nothing like that, sis."

"In love at least?"

"I'm very much in love," she answers and blows a kiss to Antonio. "What about you? Has Nacho seduced you yet?"

"Nacho?" Maria sighs. "He's fallen into the clutches of some blonde chica who sings in a country/western bar. Her name is Britney Fleming."

"Fleming? What would his mama say about that? She's definitely not the sweet Mexican girl that she wanted for her son."

"Claudia! Nacho's mama wanted one of us for her son."

"Well, he can't have me. I'm in love with Antonio."

"And I'm in love with Britney's brother."

Claudia's eyes pop open wide. Then she sighs. "Oh Maria, another Fleming? What's his name?"

"Nick. But Claude, he is so sweet, so sensitive, and so supportive. When Nacho got beat up...."

"Nacho got beat up?"

"That's right. Some deranged cowboy who's obsessed with Britney called a bunch of tough guys together, and they cornered Nacho. They beat him so badly that they almost killed him. Nick paid all the bills for his recovery. Then he went to the sheriff, said that they couldn't beat up one of his *workers* like that, and...."

"His workers?"

"Of course, he's the boss; he owns the ranch, and...."

"I see."

Claudia's voice turns cold. She listens to her sister babble on about Nick, and finally, she has to say it. "Maria, he's just using you."

"No, he's not."

"Are you sleeping with him?"

"Well only once... last night. But Claude, he loves me. You should hear the wonderful things he says to me."

"Yeah right."

"Listen, Claudia. I don't care what you say. We're in love and...."

"Marry the owner of the Rancho just like in the Telenovellas? I thought you were supposed to be the practical one, and I was the dreamer. Don't you know that gringo men will say anything to take advantage of a young woman? You sound like you think you're some princess in a Disney cartoon. Tell me, have the mice and ducks and pigs started singing to you yet, Maria? Has Nick given you love's first kiss and awakened you from your stupid fantasy?"

CLICK!

Maria suddenly hangs up the phone ending the call from her sister.

"Damn!" Claudia says. "I shouldn't have done that."

"Made fun of your sister's love life?"

"I was just trying to protect her from those users on the other side of the border."

Antonio grins, "I get the feeling that your sister can take care of herself, Claude."

"I don't know. Maybe."

"So, call her back."

Claudia stares at her lover. She shakes her head, "I can't do that." And just then the phone rings.

Slowly, she lifts the receiver to her ear, "Hola."

"I'm sorry, Claude." It's Maria.

"I am too."

"Let's not be mad at each other. I love you. You know that."

"I know, and I love you."

There's a long pause, and the sisters seem to be able to sense each other's forgiveness through the phone. Finally, Claudia calls out tearfully, "Maria, I'm calling to ask you to join us."

"What? Where?"

"We're going to the Alamo. You have to meet us there."

"Why would you ever want to do that?"

"We're making a political statement. You won't believe this Maria, but Antonio and I have put together an army, a whole army, and we're camped here, right now, at the Mexican border. Three professional soldiers have joined us and are training our troops. We even have a tank. In fact, Hector Oliva...."

"The King of Beans?"

"Junior... his son, he brought the tank. He wanted to use it to knock down the border wall right away. But I...."

"Claudia, STOP!" Maria says suddenly. "Put Antonio on the line will you, please."

"But you don't even know him."

"If he's your man, I'll know him."

Claudia turns and sees that Antonio is standing right beside her. She pushes the phone at him. "She wants to talk to you."

Antonio takes the phone. "Maria," he begins, and then he says, "I'm so happy to talk to the sister of the woman I love."

"She's crazy you know."

"Yes, I know that very well. But I love her anyway. And besides, now that Claudia's Army has formed..."

"Claudia's Army? They named an army after my crazy sister?"

"Apparently many men are in love with her, Maria. She's a strong leader, you know. They believe in her and are eager to follow her. Haven't you read the newspapers?"

"Claudia's in the newspapers?"

"There was a big picture of her on the front of the newspaper in Mexico City. Even Chubasco's little Gazette wrote about it. They say she's the Mexican Joan of Arc."

Maria shakes her head in disbelief. "So, insanity has spread throughout all of Mexico?"

"I think we should call it patriotism, Maria. Listen..." and Antonio patiently tells the story of how he, Claudia, Padre Carlos, Tío Raphael and others brought together a peasant army to act as a diversion, while a small band of warriors will make its way across the border, steal into the Alamo, and seize it.

# Chapter Twenty-Four

Appassionata Sanchez strides into the oval office looking like a starlet. She knows and understands the old man who has somehow been elected President, and she knows how to handle him. Her outfit is red, white, and blue: bright red high heels, a blue business suit with a conservative knee-length skirt, a starched white blouse, and a red scarf.

"Welcome, Appassionata," Daniel Drivel says as he rises from behind his desk and walks around to greet her. His off-target air-kiss makes a disgusting popping sound. Appassionata smiles anyway.

"Have a seat," says Drivel as he indicates a position right next to his desk. "We deployed the troops at the border just as you suggested... a couple of National Guard units."

"Very good, sir," says Sanchez. "But you understand that the main thrust will be elsewhere."

Drivel smiles for a moment and then suddenly gets very serious. "It just seems so unlikely, Appassionata. The Joint Chief's Of Staff don't think it makes any sense at all."

Sanchez nods knowingly. "It's subterfuge, sir. They think it will be too difficult to seize the real Alamo and the repercussions will be too unpopular, so instead, they are going for the replica."

She crosses her Miss Universe legs, and Drivel smiles wickedly.

"Did I ever pinch you when you were running for Miss Universe?" asks the President of The United States.

Sanchez bites her lip. "Of course not, Mr. President. That would be sexual misconduct, and you wouldn't want to be accused of that now, would you?"

"Absolutely not," says Drivel slamming his hand down hard on his desk. "Do you know what? I'm going to make you my new Communications Director."

"But sir..."

"If this invasion is all you say it is."

"It is, so thank you in advance, Mr. President."

"And, of course, I'll send the Marines to surround the Taqueria. In fact, I may even pop down there and take a look at things myself."

Sanchez beams back at The Commander and Chief.

"This is going to be a great news event for our side," he says. "We'll look like heroes; the invaders will look like blockheads."

"I don't know, Mr. President. There's something about them that's sort of..."

"Scary?"

"I was going to say AMAZING."

# Chapter Twenty-Five

"Shoulder arms!" commands Don Juan and the newest recruits to Claudia's Army make a mess of the drill.

One teenage soldier twists the rifle around so quickly that it flies up into the air, spins over his head, and falls behind him causing the troops in the second column to drop their rifles and scatter.

"Get back here, imbeciles," shouts the commander. "No one told you that you could break ranks."

Hurriedly, the recruits try to move back into position, but they're bumping into each other, tangling their rifles and their arms and legs and looking like anything but a well-trained platoon.

Beside the teenage soldier who caused all that commotion, a young man with a handlebar mustache has deftly lowered his rifle pointing the barrel out, as though it's a bayonet and he's about to charge.

"That's not what it means to shoulder arms," says Don Juan as he jerks the rifle back into the correct position.

"Shit," the young man moans.

"And that's not the proper response for a soldier in the ranks!"

From across the parade ground, Padre Carlos watches the trainees go through their exercises. He's been out here for hours, and now he shakes his head sadly at this latest display of ineptitude.

"It's a good thing we are not really going to invade," he murmurs to himself. "But for the gringos to believe we are serious we need to put on a better show than this." And he grabs a plastic folding chair and walks out into the desert as the sun begins to set.

A few minutes later, he sits, back toward the would-be soldiers, face toward the magnificent sunset.

"Dominus vobiscum, the Lord be with you," he says to no one in particular. "So, are you happy here in the desert?" he asks, then he shakes his head sadly. He knows the answer. "I didn't think so, my brothers and sisters."

"You're the souls of all those brave men and women who tried to cross this wicked desert and died trying to reach El Norte."

He nods drowsily, his head swims, and suddenly he feels he actually sees the very souls he's imagining.

They move slowly before his eyes, bowing, spinning, and whirling tragically to an unhappy waltz that seems to be carried on the wind. A handsome young man bows to the Padre. His partner, a lovely young woman with flowing hair and wide eyes, nods to the priest as well. She carries a baby. But none of them are happy. Their dance is slow and somber. Still, Padre Carlos recognizes the dancers. "Tito, Alicia!" he calls. They nod at him in recognition, and then the dance slows even more.

"Requiescat in Pace. En paz descansen," Padre Carlos whispers, "Rest in peace," and he makes the sign of the cross in the air, blessing the couple.

The ghostly man and woman cross themselves, smile weakly, and nod toward him. And suddenly they seem to be looking over his shoulder at someone else, someone behind the priest.

Carlos turns and sees Claudia walking slowing up to him.

"What are you doing out here, Padre," she asks. "Counting rattlesnakes?"

The priest shakes his head and laughs. "I was for a while. But, you know, I can't count very high. What number comes after seven hundred and fifty-four thousand?"

Claudia just smiles.

"Actually, after I gave up on my rattlesnake counting. I started praying."

"For the rattlesnakes, father?"

"No Claudia," he answers. "I'm not praying for rattlesnakes. I'm praying for the thousands of poor souls who died trying to cross this inferno with hopes for a better life... who died with their families and friends beside them, or maybe with no one but strangers nearby.

"Their relatives know they disappeared and the desert has become their burial ground. Remember the Arellano Family?"

"Of course I remember them. They were close friends of my great grandma."

"Yes, how the village mourned when we heard that all of them died trying to make it to the border. Their bodies were never found."

"No one ever really knew where they died, I guess," says Claudia, "or if, by some miracle, the reports were wrong and they made it into the north and just couldn't communicate with us any longer."

The priest shakes his head sadly. "That's the lie we all tell ourselves about the travelers. But I know the Arellanos died here. Because they were just dancing for me... dancing in death."

He gestures out to the open desert. "There. They were right there."

Claudia moves toward Padre Carlos now and studies his face. "I've had visions out here too father."

"The desert seems to be conducive to it," he answers. "Remember the gospels? And the couple in this vision were so beautiful, so graceful and lovely, but so tragic and heartbreakingly sad."

The priest gets slowly to his feet. He rests his hand on Claudia's shoulder for a moment and stares into her eyes.

"Los pinchi politicos on both sides of the border! They don't give a damn about these lost lives. Maybe we will be able to wake them up. Right?"

"That's exactly what we are going to do, father," says Claudia as she moves toward the priest and puts her arm around him. "Let's go back to the camp and get some dinner."

Carlos smiles. "Si! Cena. That would be good. I'm starving."

# Chapter Twenty-Six

Juanito trundles out of his bedroom with a backpack and his lunch box. He makes his way up to his mother and looks at her quizzically. Maria is writing a note, staring out the window from time to time, trying to find the right words. She sees her little boy and smiles.

"Where are we going, Mama?" he asks.

Maria gives him a stern look. "I told you; it's a secret."

"And it's okay that I miss school?"

Maria pulls the little boy to her and hugs him. Then she pushes him back, holds him at arm's length, and stares into his eyes.

"We're on an important and very dangerous mission," she says.

"Great, can I tell my friends?"

"No. Sorry. It has to be a secret because it's so important."

Juanito nods and grins. He likes the whole idea and his mother's serious attitude about it. He stands on tiptoes and surveys the tabletop. Several promotional folders are scattered over the surface.

"Are we going to visit the Alamo?"

Maria sighs. The letter she's writing is hard enough, and now this minor cross-examination from her little son. "Not exactly," she says.

"Does Mr. Nick know?"

"No. And I'm not going to tell him."

"Are you writing to Mr. Nick?"

Maria sighs in exasperation. "Yes. I'm writing to him."

"Well, what are you telling him?"

Maria looks heavenward in a desperate prayer for patience. Then she turns to Juanito. "I'm telling him that I'm not going to tell him where we are going."

The little boy sees the frustration in his mother's eyes. "Read it to me."

Maria smiles. "Okay, but not a word about this to anyone, understand?"

"Not even Uncle Nacho?"

"He already knows about it. He's coming with us."

The boy smiles at the news that his favorite person in the whole world will be with them. "So, let's hear it, Mama," he says.

"Okay."

*Dear Nick:*

*Juanito, Nacho, and I must go away for a few days.*

*I can't tell you why or where, all I can say is that it's very important* family business *and that we will be back very soon. I promise.*

*I love you,*

*Maria*

"That's it?" asks the boy.

Maria nods.

"Not much of a letter," he adds. "But Nick will understand, I think... I like him. Is he going to be my new father?"

Maria can't help but smile at the question. But then she gives her son a look of concern.

"Not if you tell him or anyone else where we are going."

"Will he be my new father if I don't?"

"I didn't say that." And then she smiles a radiant smile that tells her son that she does *like* the idea very much.

Juanito smiles too, and then he picks up one of the pamphlets resting on the table. He flips it over and sees a full-page ad for:

**The Alamo Taqueria**
Only twenty-six miles from the historic shrine
Just a short drive outside of town
"THE BEST TACOS IN TEXAS."

The kid holds up the ad to his mother, "Is this the place we're not exactly going to, Mama?"

\#

Nacho stands in front of Britney's little apartment. With the tender loving care of the singing cowgirl he's made a remarkable recovery. He still walks with a little limp, and he's taking heavy doses of Advil. But all in all he feels very healthy and very lucky. Besides, he thinks, the adventure that Maria described over the phone may just be the tonic he needs to become his old self again.

Now he looks down the road and spots Maria's battered old PT Cruiser rumbling toward him. She pulls up in front, rolls down the passenger side window and asks, "Got everything?"

"Si." Nacho smiles as he holds up his little backpack and his guitar. Then he spots Juanito in the back seat. He drops his gear, turns his fists into pretend pistols, and fires at the kid.

"Ka-BLAM!"

The kid draws his own imaginary guns and fires back.

"Ka-POW!"

Nacho swivels around and leans back against the railing of the apartment building. Doing it hurts him, but he still can't help but say, "You got me, bandido. I'm a dead man!"

"Nacho will you please just get into the car? I don't want to be late," Maria calls.

"Late for what? The invasion?"

"Invasion," says Juanito as his voice fills with wonder.

"We're going to pay these gringos back for the way they've treated us," says Nacho.

"Stop it!" Maria says. "This is not about payback!"

"What then?"

"Politics."

Juanito unbuckles his seatbelt and peers at his mother from behind the front seat. "What's politics, Mama?"

"Something no honest person should ever get involved in," answers Nacho.

"You mean like murder?"

Nacho laughs. "Exactly."

#

No more than fifteen minutes later, Britney Fleming pulls her bright pink jeep up in front of her condo. She pops the trunk, walks around in back, and pulls out a big bag full of groceries. It's loaded with the makings of a complete spaghetti dinner: pasta, Italian sausage, vine ripened tomatoes, garlic, oregano, olive oil, canolis, Italian bread, and a bottle of very expensive chianti.

Britney croons a soft Italian love song as she lifts the bag and carries it into her apartment.

"Nacho, I'm home," she calls as she rounds the corner into the kitchen and drops the bag onto the countertop.

"Nacho.... where are you?"

There's no answer of course. But Britney grins deciding that the big man is still asleep.

"I'm going to make a wonderful dinner for you handsome," she coos. "Gonna turn you into a Mexican Rudolph Valentino...."

She turns toward the bedroom and is surprised to see how bright it looks. The shades must be open because sunlight is streaming in through the bedroom window.

Britney runs into the room and stops in front of the bed. Nacho has made it... neatly, perfectly, only the way a man who has been well trained by his Mama ever could.

"Oh, Nacho, damn it!" she sobs and then spots a note tucked under the edge of the pillow... almost out of site.

> *Britney:*
> *Maria and I are on our way to re-capture the Alamo.*
> *Together with her sister Claudia and her little son.*
> *We are part of a great cause.*
> *It is now or never.*
> *But I still love you,*
> *Nacho*

Britney sinks onto the bed. "Oh, Nacho, now you're part of a great cause, and I'll probably never see you again."

But then she straightens. "YES I WILL." And she reaches into her jeans pocket and pulls out her cell phone. One touch of her thumb and she speed dials her brother. He answers on the first ring.

"Britney?"

"Yeah, me. Do you know anything about this trip Nacho and Maria are taking?"

Nick sighs. "I just got a note from Maria. Something about very important family business...."

"Retaking the Alamo is family business?"

"The Alamo?"

Britney laughs suddenly. "It looks like Nacho told me more than Maria told you, bro. He says they are joining a great cause... to re-capture the Alamo."

"Oh shit," Nick sighs. They can't be serious, they'll get killed."

"Who would shoot unarmed Mexicans?"

"Are you kidding, sis... tons of people."

Britney shakes her head frantically. "I don't understand any of this."

"Turn on the TV. There's something on about the Marines surrounding someplace."

"The Alamo?"

"I think they've surrounded the taqueria."

"The one outside of San Antonio?"

"Best tacos in Texas."

"But that's great food. Whoever's in charge of things has to be out of his mind."

"I think so too."

"I don't want my Nacho being assassinated. Nick! We have to do something."

"We can try to catch up with them, head them off, talk some sense into them."

"Oh God, I hope so."

"I'll be over in a few minutes. Grab some clothes and bring your guns."

"You bet I will."

"In the meantime," Nick adds, "Why don't you turn on the TV... see if you can learn any more."

"I will, Nick. But hurry."

Britney clicks off her cell phone, then stands, goes to the closet, takes out a small rolling satchel and opens it onto the bed. She glances around for things to put into it and notices the TV remote. She grabs it, turns to the TV on her dresser, and flips it on, right to CNN.

154

A hard-boiled news reporter holds a mike and addresses the camera.

*"This is Ginger Mccloskey, reporting from right outside the entrance to the Alamo Taqueria where an entire unit of the United States Marines has just arrived. They seem to be setting up defensive positions around the perimeter, but some distance from the building itself.*

*"We spoke to the manager of the restaurant, and he told me that lots of marines from the nearby reserve installation come to the restaurant all the time, that they love the place. "Perhaps," he told me, "They came for the 5 for 3 sale (Five tacos for three dollars). But that promotion is already over.*

*"On top of all that, a celebrity wedding celebration has been scheduled for this evening. Perhaps that explains what's going on."*

"What the???" whispers Britney, but she keeps packing.

# Part Three

# Chapter Twenty-Seven

Manuel Rosas marches into the building flipping on light switches as he comes. He's energetic, robust, full of life, almost seventy years old and yet he has easily finished the daily two-mile run from his home to his sprawling Mexican restaurant. He'll take his morning shower after the rest of the crew arrives. In the meantime, someone has to get his business started for the day, and he takes great pride in doing it himself.

He enters through the back door, and it's quite a hike just to get to the front: through the food storage area, food preparation, through the double doors into the vast dining room with all the booths and tables. Then, down another hallway, past the gift shop overflowing with souvenir towels, t-shirts, mugs, and post cards. He stops, stretches, and moves on.

Near the very front of the building, he glances to the left and sees what is now only a small room. But once it was the whole place, the actual, authentic Taqueria that his parents started so many years ago. This vast complex that Manuel now runs has been added onto it.

Manuel sighs. In spite of his high energy, he is a sentimental man, and so he keeps the original Taqueria open every day. And it has plenty of customers. But now the place has grown to be so much more than the small Taqueria his parents opened with his sisters and brothers. Manuel knows the exact date it all started. He strides into the wide hallway leading from the front door and into the waiting area. Just behind the hostess podium with its little "Welcome," sign, hangs an enormous oil portrait of Juventino Rosas, the great Mexican classical composer, and Manuel's great, great uncle.

In 1888, Juventino wrote what is perhaps the most famous waltz ever written by someone who was not from Vienna and not named Strauss. His piece, 'Over The Waves', was an international success, a hit recording sung by Mario Lanza, and a standard on every carousel ever made.

Manuel closes his eyes for a moment and hears the music, feels the whirling of his first carousel ride, and sees the little amusement park, here in Mole Texas just outside of San Antonio. His parents Salvador and Fabiola brought him and his brother Kiki and his little sisters Julia and Patricia to spend the day. They had decided to take a chance in the Mexican food business, and, when Mama Fabiola saw the carousel and heard it playing her uncle's famous waltz, she felt it was a sign from heaven.

"We must live here," she told Papa Salvador as they sat amid the crowds in the park eating ice cream and watching the children ride the merry-go-round.

"In Mole?"

"Why not? What better place to make great Mexican food? After all, the town is named for a sauce."

"Mole sauce," Papa Salvador confirmed. And just then little Patricia came running up to them.

"Papa, can we stay here?" she begged.

"At the park? I'm afraid we have to leave soon."

"But I want to stay here forever, Papa."

"I told you so," giggled Fabiola as she batted those long irresistible eyelashes of hers, and what could Salvador do? She looked so very lovely that he had to say, "Yes. I guess this will be our home."

Manuel had witnessed the whole conversation, and he was glad. Mole Texas seemed like the perfect place for them. And now, decades later as he remembers it all, he runs his finger across the bottom of the great golden picture frame holding the portrait of the great composer, his Uncle Juventino. "Clean as a whistle," he murmurs, and he smiles.

The wall along the hallway that leads from the Welcome area to the front door, features a row of photographs that portray the restaurant's history.

The first photo nearest to the great portrait shows the old storefront Papa Salvador rented. The whole family worked there, Manuel remembers. They sold masa for tortillas and tamales. He steps to the next photo. There he is, fourteen years old, working beside his sisters making masa, hands up to his elbows mixing the cornmeal. He looks so serious, Manuel thinks, working so hard, making such a high-quality product.

A step past the factory images and there's the Taqueria that the family opened: Papa Salvador and Mama Fabiola now quite a bit older, posing outside the little building. A banner hangs across the front announcing:

BEST TACOS IN TEXAS!

Now come the sports photos: the champion soccer teams that the Rosas family sponsored.

Next picture: Salvador and Fabiola retiring, a big picnic in the parking lot, family, friends, Father Ramirez is standing toasting Mama and Papa. What a happy day.

Manuel moves forward, and then he sighs again. Here it is, the moment that started the great expansion: a photo of movie star

160

Wayne Duke sitting inside the little taqueria smiling broadly, holding up a beer and one of Mama Fabiola's signature Tacos.

"I'll tell the world," says Wayne. And he does, at least everyone on the set of the movie, THE BATTLE FOR THE ALAMO.

From there, the number of pictures on the wall expands significantly: a wrap party featuring the entire cast of the movie. Tony Pedroya, who played Santa Anna, stands before dozens of picnic tables loaded with Mexican food.

Next, come images of the construction site: the expanded Taqueria being created to resemble the famous landmark. There are bulldozers in action, painters and construction workers, Sal, Manuel, and Kiki together joking with Wayne Duke who keeps visiting during the construction. Patricia, Fabiola, and Rita cut the ribbon on the front door, the one designed to look like the entrance to the famous mission.

The pictures get even better: Miguel serves tacos to Hall of Fame Quarterback Dandy Don Kingston. Kiki entertains the Dallas Cowboy Cheerleaders, each of whom is holding one of the "BEST TACOS IN TEXAS." Governor Walt Johnson sits in the original taqueria, napkin tucked into his collar, eating a huge burrito, and giving a big thumbs-up.


"Are you looking at those old photos again, Pops," asks a sweet voice.

"Of course, darling," says Miguel, and he opens his arms for his oldest daughter, Emma. She hugs him, then looks him in the eyes and says, "Only a few more days, huh?"

Miguel nods.

"You'll be around a lot though," Emma adds. "We can't keep grandma and grandpa away, and I'm sure you and Mom will be here too."

"Once we get back from this damn European trip," Miguel says almost regretfully.

"Come on, Pops, you'll love Italy and Spain."

"Okay, I'll enjoy it, I promise."

"You owe it to Mama."

"Yeah, I do," says Miguel. "Can't imagine much more could happen to the old place anyway," adds Miguel as he pats the friendly wall beside the front door.

"Oh, I don't know about that," answers Emma.

# Chapter Twenty-Eight

"We are here to take back our lands! To take back what rightfully belongs to Mexico," the Prince of Beans, Hector Oliva Junior, shouts to everyone within earshot. He stands atop his father's tank directing his driver to plow all along the unfinished sections of the border wall. Sancho, his driver, is as excited as the prince. He veers brazenly toward the American troops on the other side then jerks the tank away at the last minute.

"We will push you back! Push you back! Waaaay back!" taunts Hector Junior. "We will pulverize your wall and see that it never rises again."

"The kid is nuts," says Antonio. He and Tío Rafael and Padre Carlos stand on a makeshift platform they use as a reviewing stand. One of Don Juan's fellow regular army buddies drills the very best troops of Claudia's Army on the field in front of them. Hector and his tank swerve wildly along in the distance.

"This platoon looks damn professional," says Rafael.

"The best we have," answers Antonio. "Mostly former soldiers and kids with an aptitude for the military."

"I have to admit you manage to put on quite a show," laughs Padre Carlos.

"Wonderful distraction," says Tío Rafael.

"And this is just the beginning," says Antonio. "Just wait."

Less than a quarter of a mile away, on the US side, General Bradley Oldman watches the action with unbelieving eyes. At age 67, he is currently the oldest person on active duty in the armed forces. Of course, he's lived with the name Oldman all his life and was called OLD MAN even when he was in grade school. "Here comes the old man," kids would call, and for a while young Brad Oldman played along with it, adopting a hobbling walk and a bent over posture to add to the joke. Now, he prides himself on being fit, jogging six miles every day, working out in the weight room five days a week. And he is especially proud of his ramrod straight posture. But sometimes his 1960's speech dates him.

"Where'd they get that awesome tank?" he asks his adjutant, Lieutenant Mona Esposito. She shrugs. "Looks like it's Russian-made."

"Far Out. Bet it came from one of those bad ass drug cartels."

"Wouldn't make sense, would it, boss?" asks Mona, "The cartels thrive on the confusion of international policies. Why would they help one side or the other?"

Oldman glances back at his aide; she's third generation Mexican American: hair pulled back in a tight bun, slim-fitting Army camo gear, and a rugged expression on her face. She's probably no more than twenty-five, he thinks, but he knows she's smarter than he is... and tougher too. She beats him regularly at arm wrestling.

"So then where did it come from?" he asks.

"New model, crazy kid driving it? He looks like the son of that BEAN guy, The King of Beans... probably bought it to protect some of his remote holdings."

"And just why would he do that?"

"To intimidate the locals and his rivals. Certainly, no one is going to give him any shit."

Now, on the Mexican side, the troops on the parade ground make an abrupt turn toward the border. Armed soldiers move up behind them, some in camo from what looks like army surplus stores, others in jeans and cotton shirts with logos sewn onto the sleeves. They are all armed, those in the first ranks with rifles and machine guns, those behind them with pistols and grenade launchers.

Oldman studies the troops with his binoculars. Those at the very front are young and tough. They look intent and dedicated. Those behind them are older. Some appear to be former assembly line workers from the now-defunct auto plant; a few look like college kids.

"So where'd they get those righteous weapons and uniforms?"

"Probably from the same guy who gave them the tank," says Esposito.

"The King of Beans?"

"El Rey del Frijol, yes, sir."

The general turns toward his own troops: National Guard units from all over Texas are backing up dozens of agents from the border patrol. He has about five hundred personnel in all... facing over a thousand.

Further into the Texas desert are vigilante groups comprising a disorganized cadre of maybe two hundred more men and women. They bring their own weapons and rides: choppers, trucks of every size and make. Right now they are treating the whole event like a picnic, serving up barbeque, beans, and beer. But Oldman knows it won't take much to get them moving, to have them hop into their vehicles and charge across the border, ready for all-out vigilante warfare.

"Isn't that an honest-ta-god rocket launcher?" Oldman asks.

"No doubt about it, sir," says Esposito.

"They make one wrong move, and we blast em. Understand?"

"Yes sir."


And now, from far away on the Mexican side, the general hears a wild Mexican Grito as several hundred more peasants come rushing out of the nearby desert. They carry hoes, pitchforks, knives, and are ready to join the invasion.

"Claudia's Army," says Mona Esposito with a grimace.

"Outta sight!"

"Yes, sir."

"And just which retard is in charge a' that operation?"

Oldman scans the troops and spots Don Juan rumbling beside the advancing soldiers in a Hummer. He's doing his best to give direction to the various units. Beside him, her hair swirling in the wind is Claudia, bandoliers crisscrossed over her chest outlining her proud and defiant figure.

"Claudia," answers his aide.

"She is CHOICE," Oldman grunts.

"I think so too, general," adds Mona. "But Don Juan Rodriquez is a former commander in the Mexican Army, and he's the guy running this part of the mission."

"You mean there are *other* friggin parts?"

"Almost certainly, sir," says Mona with a disconcerting smirk. "Almost certainly."

"Bummer."

# Chapter Twenty-Nine

The tire explodes with the force of cannon fire, and Clayton Bailey's big Ram pickup swerves wildly toward the edge of the road.

"Whoa, there," groans the Lone Stranger as he fights for control of his ride. "Don't fail me now, old hoss."

But the Ram does. Jerking control away from the crazy cowboy, it plows off the highway, down into a gully, and then up the other side. Except it doesn't quite make it. Instead, it comes to rest halfway up the embankment, nose up, the force of gravity holding the pickup's two huge front doors tightly shut, defying anyone to try and force them open and get out... whether he's wearing a mask or not.

"TORONTO!" bellows the Lone Stranger. "Where's my faithful Canadian nephew when I need him?"

Unfortunately for the masked man, Toronto is far away, forgetting the Texas heat and enjoying the rest of a balmy Canadian summer.

Bailey slams his shoulder against the huge door and gets it open just enough so that he can squeeze through it.

"Mother of Cheese," curses the mask man as he hobbles around the back of the truck. He reaches into the bed and pulls out a saddlebag containing his twin pistols, his gun belts, and his rifle.

"Stay put, old hoss," mumbles Bailey as he slings the saddlebag over his shoulder, stumbles away from the crippled vehicle and begins making his way up to the side of the road.

No sooner had he reached the edge of the highway than an old Volkswagen bus pulls up in front of him and stops. It's painted bright orange, yellow, and day-glow green with huge flowers and psychedelic themes reminiscent of the1960s.

Bailey stares at it in confusion for a few seconds, and then the driver's window rolls down, and a starry-eyed flower child smiles at him and shouts, "Hey there, cowboy, going to the Alamo? Taqueria?"

"That the place that's gonna be recaptured?" asks Bailey.

"According to the news," said the young woman.

"Then yes... yes I am."

She turns to her companions and speaks to them for a minute, then looks at Bailey, grins, and says, "Hop in Cowboy. There's always room for someone willing to fight for the rights of the migrants."

Bailey stiffens for a moment trying to figure out if these kids and he are on the same wavelength... let alone the same side. They never have been before, but on the other hand he really needs a ride. So he curses under his breath and makes his way to the van's big rear door.

"I'm Moonglow," smiles a pretty brunette in a fringed vest and hip hugger jeans as she opens the door. "You look just like the cowboy in that Johnny Depp movie. The one where Johnny plays the Indian."

"Box office failure," mumbles Bailey as he reaches forward and lets Moonglow and her friends pull him onto the bus.

Three young women and two young men cluster around Bailey. Each sports a big grin, crazy eyes, and marijuana breath.

"Yo, Dude," said a dark skinned kid, "My name's Earl Whitney."

Bailey reached forward to take the kid's hand and finds his own fist bumped, twisted, and exploded into a complex handshake that seems to be totally out of his control.

"Glad to have you aboard, I'm Ronny," says a second young man who puts his arm over Earl's shoulder and hugs him.

"You two together?" asks Bailey.

"Husband and wife," answers Earl.

"Two guys married?"

"Deeply in love," answers Earl. "And by the way those are some cool duds you're wearing there. You're impersonating the Lone Ranger, right?"

"Course not, says Ron. "The lone ranger wears *powder* blue. This guy has on *baby* blue. What's wrong with you, sweetheart?"

"Damn," says Earl, "How could I have missed that?"

"So if you're not the Lone Ranger," says Moonglow, "You must be..."

"The Lone Stranger," answers Bailey.

"Cute. And how do you like our banner, Mr. Stranger?" asks Crystal, another of the young women.

"What banner is that?"

"The one on the passenger side of the van."

Bailey looks stumped for a moment and only then does Earl say, "Hey girl, it's on the *other side of the bus*. He couldn't see it from where he was."

"What's it say?" asks Bailey.

"WHAT BORDER?"

"As in, '*we don't need no stinkin' border*,'" says Ron, doing a bad impression of the famous movie line."

The others all laugh. Even Bailey gets it.

"Claudia and her army are trying to redress a terrible wrong," says Moonglow.

Earl says, "You know... the immigration policies and all that?"

Crystal says, "The crap that guy in the White House keeps spouting."

"You don't agree with any a that shit, do you, Lone Stranger?"

Bailey checks out the slightly stoned faces of the kids who have just rescued him.

"Where are you heading?" he asks.

"To the support rally," answers, Ron, "Right near the Alamo Taqueria."

"Within shouting distance," says Moonglow.

"Within *shooting* distance," murmurs Bailey, but no one hears him.

"I understand there are hundreds of Claudia's supporters there, ready to add their voices in protest."

Bailey smiles. "I'd like to attend the rally."

"Sure," says Moonglow, "As long as you're coming to help the migrants in their fight for fair access to jobs in America."

"Don't be silly," says Earl, "Who wouldn't support them?"

"Right," echoes Bailey, "Who wouldn't support them?"

He strokes his rifle angrily... but then he smiles.

# Chapter Thirty

The sun is setting as Maria steers her little car off to the side of the road.

"I'm so tired," she sighs, "All the preparation, stress, driving."

She closes her eyes to squeeze out the tears that have begun to form. And that's when she feels a big soft hand caressing her shoulder.

"Don't cry, Maria," whispers Nacho. "It's alright."

His touch is as gentle as Maria remembers from their childhood play. Even when games were rough, he treated the girls tenderly. And his voice was always so reassuring... as it is now.

"I can drive," he says. "Let's all switch places. You just curl up in the back seat, and I'll get us there."

Maria pulls herself from behind the wheel and walks slowly around to the passenger side. Juanito gets out and helps her into the back. Then he moves into the front, while Nacho climbs into the drivers seat.

The big man turns, gives the kid a high five, and, of course, adds "Ka-BLAM!"

He takes the Alamo pamphlet from the dashboard for a moment and studies it. "This is all very clear," he says as he flips from one page to the other.

"And wow, it's quite a place, boys and girls, let me tell you. I am impressed that we built such a great mission so that it could become a historic symbol of someone else's country."

Juanito giggles. Maria does too, and the next sound they hear from her is gentle snoring.


The PT Cruiser comes to a crossroads.

"To the left," calls Juanito, "And quick; there's a motorcade coming."

Nacho looks that way, sees a grand parade of cars moving slowly along the highway, and realizes that it's too late. Their little car begins shaking with the sound of horns blaring, motors rumbling, voices shouting and cheering, headlights glaring. Men and women in formal clothes – some in tuxedos and ball gowns – lean out of car windows waving and cheering. In the first car, a convertible with its top down, is a large man. He's standing up, leaning over the front windshield, waving a huge cowboy hat in celebration. Alongside the convertible rolls a TV truck. A video camera mounted on the roof follows the action. There's a big satellite dish pointing skyward from behind it. Other paparazzi ride along on motorbikes. Shooters in sidecars lean from their cycles and take snapshots of the parade.

"What did I tell you?" says Nacho with a broad grin. "They are on their way to the recapturing. That Claudia! What a woman."

"Let's get down there," he adds. "Let's join the celebration."

"But Nacho," says Juanito, "I'm looking at the map, the Alamo is the other way it's in San Antonio. They are heading to a little town called... Mole?"

"Of course they are. They need to pass through the place named for the greatest sauce in the world."

"Uh, I think it's actually named after a gopher," answers the kid. "Besides these people look like they are going to a wedding."

Nacho eyes the blur of partiers going by. "Silly boy," he says, "That's the way everyone dresses for a revolution."

"Really?"

"Of course, and Ka-BLAM!" And Nacho pretends to shoot the boy with his finger. "Trust your elders, Juanito."

The boy smiles at his hero and nods.

Soon Nacho has managed to work the cruiser into the line of cars and landed right behind the big convertible. The motorcade breasts a rise, and suddenly Nacho, the boy, and even the awakening Maria are astounded at the view. The Alamo, or maybe a replica of the historic shrine, lies nestled in the valley before them.

"We are in luck Amigos!" Nacho shouts. "Look. The Alamo serves food."

And, sure enough, just below a big neon sign on the front of the building announcing THE ALAMO, is the word TAQUERIA. It lights up in counterpoint to the name, in equally bright letters.

THE ALAMO
TAQUERIA
THE ALAMO
TAQUERIA

Directly in front of the main entryway to the Alamo (Taqueria), bathed in a pool of light, reporters from Entertainment Tonight face the TV cameras.

Nacho grins like a tourist, and his smile grows even wider as he sees famed Comedian Frankie Lopez step out of the passenger side of the convertible.

173

"Dios Mio," cries Nacho. "Even Hollywood has joined the fight. I tell you, Maria, your sister is a wonder woman."

"Uh, maybe not," adds Maria. "This seems more like a wedding reception than a battle."

And they all look on as Lopez opens the back door of the convertible and a handsome couple steps out: a young woman in a magnificent wedding gown accompanies a good-looking young Latino in a tux and tails. The comedian leads them to the spotlight where the reporters are waiting to interview them all.

Suddenly, there's a rap on the window of Maria's little car. It's a security guard. Maria rolls down her back window and the guard goes to talk to her.

"Excuse me, folks," he says politely. "Can I see your invitation?"

Maria bites her lip and stares nervously back and him.

She seems very sweet and shy, the guard thinks. But still, he has to do his job.

"Are you members of the Mexican Wedding Party?" he asks.

Maria does not answer. But Nacho does.

"Of course," he says. "We are Mexicans, and we love to party."

The guard laughs. "Regretfully, that may not be enough to get you...."

"What's going on, Max?" a friendly voice interrupts.

"Señor Frankie Lopez," Nacho announces to everyone within earshot as the TV star approaches.

Nacho gets out of the car. He wears workmen's clothes and big boots, not especially appropriate for a battle but even less appropriate for a wedding.

The comedian looks him up and down. "You want to attend my daughter's wedding reception, Mr..."

"Gonzales," Nacho answers proudly, "Francisco Alfredo Gonzales Gonzales Gonzales. But you can call me Nacho."

"Greetings, Nacho. Are you friends of the groom?"

"Is his name Gonzales Gonzales Gonzales?" asks Nacho with a big grin.

Lopez thinks for a moment and then shrugs, "Well, he's 'Gonzales Gonzales,' anyway."

"Then he's my second cousin!"

Lopez smiles. "Wonderful! Bien venidos to our wedding reception. We're glad you could make it. Welcome to the Alamo Taqueria."

Nacho's smile fades. "So this is NOT the authentic, actual, real Alamo, Señor?"

Lopez shakes his head.

"Just a moment then," Nacho says, "I need to talk to my friend here."

Frankie Lopez sees Maria looking at them through the window, and nods to her. She gives him her warmest smile.

"Your friend is lovely Nacho," says Lopez. "In fact, she looks very familiar."

Maria hears the words and feels a little frightened. She eyes the guards and police working the function, and then glances nervously at Nacho. But he only says Ka-BLAM! and turns back to Lopez.

"Have you been to The Guadalajara Mariachi Festival, Señor?" he asks.

The comedian grins broadly and pats him on the back. "That's some Fiesta eh, amigo. My whole family goes every year."

"Yes," responds Nacho, "there's no better place to experience the Mariachi tradition than the festival: religious services with Mariachi performances, parades with Mariachi floats, folk ballets, art exhibits and the largest Mariachi competition in the world."

"You sound like a TV ad," says Lopez.

"Ah, but that's where you saw our lovely Maria and her sister. They competed as part of Los Tigres Musicales, one of the greatest of all Mariachi groups."

"Really?" asks Lopez.

"Si," but Nacho isn't content to end it there. "To think how it all started," he adds dramatically. "Would you like to know?"

Lopez glances over his shoulder at the long line of cars that is slowly moving toward the entrance to the restaurant. "Unfortunately...."

"You are right about that," Nacho continues. "It WAS unfortunate."

The big man is inspired now. He reaches into the back of the little cruiser and pulls out his guitar. "May I play something for you, Señior Lopez?"

The TV star looks around desperately for the security guard. He spots him standing a short distance away chatting with a friend.

"Max," says Lopez. "Please let Mr. Gonzales Gonzales Gonzales and his family into the reception," Then he turns to Maria, "See you inside, Señora." And he walks back to the line of cars.

# Chapter Thirty-One

More quickly than they would have expected, Manuel Rosas himself, the soon-to-retire owner of The Alamo Taqueria, leads Nacho, Maria, and Juanito to a large booth in the great dining room.

"I believe someone is expecting you," says Manuel as they approach.

"Ka-BLAM," shouts Nacho in astonishment. There in the booth, looking as lovely as the songs she sings, is Britney Fleming.

Nacho rushes to her and slides in beside her.

"You shouldn't be here," he says.

"Hey, like this is one of my favorite restaurants in all of Texas," answers Britney, and she blows a kiss to Manuel as he helps Maria and Juanito into the booth.

"Okay," says Manuel. "It looks like you guys are all set. Whenever you're ready, get in line for your comida."

"Miss Britney, this is not your fight," Nacho whispers too loudly. "Only Mexicans are allowed."

"I saw the news and heard the reporters," she answers, "Something about a woman named Claudia and her army, and the border wall. But what's that got to do with this place... and this wedding reception?"

"I don't know much about it myself," Nacho answers. "But it's only for Mexicans."

Britney suddenly gets a big smile. "Well, I'm part Mexican because I love mariachi music, and I can speak perfect Mexican."

Nacho nods. "Yes, you can."

"And I love the taste of a nice, big, juicy enchilada."

Nacho stares at Maria who smirks and just shrugs.

"So I'm sure there must be a lot of Mexican in me."

Nacho smiles. "Okay, you can stay, mi angel. Because of the part of you that's Mexican... but especially because of the part of you that's a crack shot."

"Ka-BLAM," says the singing cowgirl, and she winks at him.

"Ka-BLAM?" asks Nick as he makes his way back to the booth. And then he spots Maria. He doesn't say another word just slides in beside her and takes her hand.

There's a moment of silence while Nacho stares at Britney and Nick looks lovingly at Maria. "Mush," moans Juanito as he jumps up from the table, "I'm gonna get some food."

"Okay," says Maria, "Just don't take more than you can eat."

"Yes, Mom."

Maria turns to Nick as her son heads toward the food line. "But how did you get here?"

"We heard about the upcoming battle and we knew that's where you were headed," says Nick.

"But I didn't tell you anything."

Britney giggles. "No, but Nacho did. We've been coming to this restaurant all our lives. Nick knows a back way, and he got us here in half the time."

"So," Nick says to Maria, "What is this really all about?"

Maria eyes Nacho as though seeking his permission to tell the whole story.

Nacho nods, and so Maria tells as much as she knows, starting with the attempt to cross the border, and Tío Joaquín's injury.

"And so that's how we all ended up here, at a wedding reception in the Alamo Taqueria?" asks Britney.

"According to my sister and CNN," says Maria.

Nick nods but just has to ask, "So, how is your uncle?"

Maria sighs and looks very sad. "Not well, of course. And this upcoming battle seems to be about so much more than his health."

"No one has enough money to pay for his operation," adds Nacho.

"Claudia told me that there are plans to send him to stay with his son in Arizpe, Sonora," Maria says. "His son, Arnoldo and his wife and children have a pretty successful agricultural business there."

"So, then they can pay for the operation," says Nick.

"Maybe not, but Tío Joaquín's whole family is there," says Maria. "At least he will have plenty of attention."

Nick stares at Maria for a long moment, and then he pounds his fist on the table.

"Damn," he says.

Everyone else in the restaurant turns toward him. Finally, Nacho nods to the others and shrugs, and eventually the others all turn away.

"I'm not going to let MY uncle suffer because his family can't afford an operation," says Nick.

"YOUR uncle?" says Maria, her eyes growing wide.

"Of course," Nick answers.

"What's he talking about?" asks Nacho.

Britney giggles. "When he marries Maria, Tío Joaquín will be *his* uncle too. Isn't that how it works?"

"Marry?" asks Maria. She's stunned.

"I have a ring already picked out," Nick says, "pending your approval, of course."

"Of course," whispers Maria, afraid to say anything out loud in case she misunderstands, or this is all really just a daydream.

Nick pulls her to him and kisses her just as Juanito returns with a plate full of food. The little boy sees the kiss, gets a disgusted look on his face, moans, and turns back to the serving table to get more of something... anything.

"Doesn't your little boy approve of us?" asks Nick.

"It's more that he doesn't approve of kissing," laughs Nacho.

"Well, he'd better get used to it," adds Maria.

Britny giggles. Then maybe for no other reason than to break the mood so that Juanito can come back to the table, Britney turns to Maria and asks, "So, when will we meet your sister... the famous Claudia?"

Maria shakes her head. "I don't know where she is. I'm worried. I thought she'd meet us here. You don't suppose the Marines have captured her?"

Nacho laughs. "Claudia is too smart and too crazy, Miha. They aren't going to catch her."

Maria nods. Then she takes Nicks hand and kisses it. "I'm so happy," she says. "I just don't want anything to go wrong. Claudia just has to be all right.

"But where is she?"

# Chapter Thirty-Two

The real Alamo sleeps peacefully in the Texas night. Stars twinkle. The place is about to close. That's when the invaders arrive in a little Chevrolet mini-bus. They pull up to the side entrance and sneak in.

Linda Rhinestone, former Grand Ole Opry backup singer and now head cashier at the little gift shop, watches as the members of the party enter and draw their guns.

She pulls her cell phone from her pocket and types in a brief text.

"BANDIDOS with guns! Come quickly."

"Interesting place," says Padre Carlos, as he stands in the fabled courtyard. Somehow he seems able to feel the terrible events of the past.

"So many brave men died here," says Claudia.

"On both sides," adds Antonio, and then he spots a bit of light coming from the gift shop.

He strides over to the door and pushes it open.

"I claim this shrine in the name of the people of Mexico!"

"Oh, really," says Linda as she stands at the cash register closing out for the night. "Isn't it a little late for that?"

"The time could never be more appropriate."

Linda eyes him and carefully locks the cash register.

"I suppose you have an army with you," she says.

"Who needs an army," answers Antonio. "All we want is publicity."

Linda rolls her eyes. "You and everyone else. Except at my age, any publicity I get will be too late."

"Then join our cause," says Claudia as she moves gracefully into the room and smiles at the older woman.

"I know you," Linda responds. "I've seen your pictures in the newspaper. You're the girl with the tank... on the border. What are you doing *here*?"

Antonio answers. "I told you. We've come to take over this place, hold it hostage for the people of Mexico... until your President (and I use that word with much regret) comes to his senses."

Linda shrugs. "Don't hold your breath."

Suddenly, Charlie McKeever, a short, muscular, round-faced security guard, bursts into the shop, pistol drawn. He points his gun at Antonio and Claudia.

"Drop your weapons, folks."

Antonio places his pistol on the counter. Claudia pulls two revolvers from her holsters, bends forward and sets them onto the floor. Then she takes a big step backward.

"So, what's this all about?" Charlie asks. "You kids look nice enough."

"We *are* nice," says Claudia. "We're merely here to raise awareness of the situation on our border."

"You mean the American immigration policies and all that?"

"That's right," answers Claudia.

"Can't see how taking over a National Monument is going to do anything but turn people against you."

"Controversy is good," says Antonio.

"We may make people angry, but at least they'll pay attention," adds Claudia.

182

NICK IUPPA & JOHN PESQUEIRA

"Listen," says Charlie, "I've been hired to keep this place secure. Nobody is going to take it and hold it hostage on my watch.

"Linda, call central security and get a few more guys in here."

Linda stands behind her cash register and just looks at him.

"Linda?"

"Haven't you been reading about these two in the newspapers and on the Internet?"

"Maybe... maybe not. But this is a national shrine... to liberty."

"And whose liberty would that be, Señor?" asks Claudia.

Charlie turns his gun directly toward her. "I'm just doin' my job, Miss. You have to understand that."

"You and Adolf Eichmann?"

Those words come from the doorway and Padre Carlos.

"Who in the fuck is Adolf Eichmann," asks Charlie before he realizes that the statement came from a priest. Then he lowers his eyes and his gun. "Oh, sorry, Father."

Padre Carlos walks into the shop and right up to Charlie.

"Are you a good Catholic, my son?"

"Of course, Father. I'm Irish as the day is long."

"God, then give me your gun."

Yes sir," says the guard. And he humbly hands his weapon to the priest.


"Let's go up onto the wall," says the Antonio. "Let's take a look at the surrounding area. Get the lay of the land."

"We also have to raise the Mexican flag over this symbol of suffering and freedom," adds the padre.

"Take some selfies too while you're up there," says Linda. "Almost everyone does."

So, the little band of invaders does it all. They tie Charlie up, then follow Linda onto the wall and raise the flag of Mexico above the historic edifice.

"When they spot the flag in the morning," Padre Carlos says, "the press will begin to gather. The police will come too."

"Better tie me up," suggests Linda. "I might lose my job when the boss finds out that I helped you claim this shrine for a foreign power. But if ruffling a few feathers will help lead to a little more sanity in Washington, and along this border, then I'm in."

"I don't think you understand just how deeply the insanity and hatred run," says Claudia. "We were trying to cross the border only a few weeks ago, my old uncle and I, when suddenly some vigilantes shot him. They wounded the poor old man. His family is taking care of him now, and he may never walk again."

"Oh, I understand the feelings," says Linda. "I live with it believe me. Now take your pictures or whatever you need to do. Send them back to your family and friends. I think this place is going to be surrounded by all kinds of photographers and police and maybe even the National Park Service in the morning. So you'd better enjoy the peace and quiet while it lasts."

# Chapter Thirty-Three

"This is Commander Chuck Hardesty of the United States Marines. We have the place surrounded. Come out with your hands up."

The words blast in from the front of the Alamo Taqueria. The microphones in the restaurant's various rooms pick them up and relay them through the world-class speaker system. They crackle across the PAs, and everyone hears them. Wedding guests look up from the food line and from the many tables. Some people think it's a joke and begin to laugh; others are confused, worried, scared.

Frankie Lopez quickly makes his way to Maria's table. "So that's where I've seen you before, Señora."

Nacho stands, "But Frankie, remember Guadalajara, the Mariachi Festival?"

Lopez holds up his hands to silence him. "Nice try, Nacho." Then he turns to Maria. "I recognize your picture from the Mexican newspapers. They show a peasant Army massing at the border, threatening to attack. There's a tank driving back and forth along the wall. And you were there too."

Maria sits in stunned silence. She knows very little of this. She reflects for a moment, then looks up proudly and says. "It wasn't me. It was my sister, Claudia."

Lopez is thoughtful for a moment then nods, "Yes, one report referred to Claudia's Army, a band of warriors massing on the border... protesting the wall."

"I think that's what they're up to," says Nacho. "We don't have all the details either."

"I support them," says Lopez as his mouth sets into a determined line. "I even admire them. But you say they are planning to try and seize this restaurant?"

Nacho shrugs. "I guess so."

Lopez shakes his head. "So the Marines are here because of your little invasion."

"Perhaps there's another reason," sighs Nacho.

Britney adds, "I can think of one reason why the Marines would lay siege to a taqueria."

Everyone turns to her. "Why?"

"There's really great food!"

Lopez breaks into laughter and has to fight to control himself. Finally, he looks from Maria to Nacho to Juanito to Nick and Britney and then back to Nacho. He shakes his head again. "We have to face this commander, amigos. One of you better come with me."


Moments later, Lopez and Nacho step out of the restaurant and move toward a massive trailer pulled off to the side of the entryway. It's the Marines Tactical Operations Center. Nacho is waving a white t-shirt that he grabbed from the restaurant gift shop. It's on the end of another souvenir, a long plastic sword.

As they approach, the loud speakers from the van call out, "Who goes there?"

"Representatives of the wedding party," Lopez calls back.

There's a moment of silence, and then Commander Chuck Hardesty steps out of the trailer with two rifle-carrying guards beside him. The three men are enormous, muscular, wearing desert camo fatigues and high lace-up boots. As tall as Nacho is, these men tower over him.

They arrive at a spot half way between the van and the entrance to the taqueria. Suddenly a blinding circle of light illuminates them all. Flashlights pop everywhere. The press is there too, and they want to follow the exchange.

The commander stares at Lopez for a moment and then announces, "You are under arrest by order of The President of the United States. So is everyone in that building. We have orders to recapture this taqueria and hold it."

Lopez can't help smiling. "Who are you holding it from?"

Hardesty stares intently at the comedian. He sees no humor in the situation at all. "The Mexicans."

Lopez continues to smile as though the big guys with the guns are just hecklers in some Miami nightclub. "Almost all of us are Mexican, Señor. What have we done wrong?"

Again Hardesty's answers are all business. "You invaded US territory for political purposes."

"How could we invade? I was born here. I'm an American. Plus I put down a very hefty deposit. I reserved the taqueria and its services to celebrate my daughter's wedding."

Hardesty doesn't answer; he just stares at Frankie.

Lopez stares back. Finally, he asks, "When did your family arrive in this country, Commander?"

The soldier doesn't answer for a long time and then finally shrugs. "I guess Uncle Harry and Aunt Maude came over after the potato famine in 1916."

Lopez smiles. "We came here so long ago that we don't even remember. There was no American History back then. Maybe it was 1066."

One of the two guards turns to Hardesty and whispers, "The Battle of Hastings, sir."

"Just an unimportant date I learned in school," Lopez adds. "Not sure what it has to do with the history of the American Southwest, but they taught it to us anyway."

"And where do you think those potatoes came from, Commander... the ones that saved your people?" Nacho asks, but Frankie Lopez grabs him by the arm and squeezes.

"This time, be quiet, Nacho," he whispers.

So, the five men stand there staring at each other until Frankie Lopez gives a benevolent smile.

"I have an idea, Commander. Why don't you and your brave Marines come in and share our wedding feast?"

"Best Tacos in Texas," Nacho adds.

"My orders are from the President of the United States, and he commands us to seize the Alamo Taqueria and arrest everyone inside."

"What a way to ruin a party," says Nacho.

Frankie Lopez now steps in front of Nacho and still smiling adds, "Okay, if you want to arrest everyone, Commander, go ahead and do it. But remember you'll be arresting all of my Mexican friends, my gringo friends, the Archbishop of San Antonio, the Mayor of Guadalajara, and my Uncle Alfonzo who has a grave heart condition."

Again there is silence. Hardesty is stoic, unblinking. Finally, he says. "I'll run this up the chain of command. Get further instructions. But in the mean time, I warn you, anyone who tries to leave will be shot."

Nacho can't hold back any longer. He steps up beside Lopez, pulls the t-shirt off of his plastic souvenir sword and draws a line in the sand.

"So everyone must leave now or die?"

Hardesty just rolls his eyes and shakes his head. "I just told you NO ONE can leave. No swords, no lines in the sand. Leave all that stuff to the movies."

"The Alamo," says Nacho.

"What about it?" asks the Commander.

"That's the movie where Colonel William B. Travis drew a line in the sand with his sword. 'Those who would fight to the death cross over but those who would live better fly'."

"Really?" asks Lopez.

"If you don't believe me rent the DVD."

"No lines in the sand," grumbles Hardesty. "No one leaves."

"Okay, good," says Nacho.

" You think that's good?" asks Lopez.

"Well, it's okay. I broke my sword and can't draw any more lines in the sand anyway."

# Chapter Thirty-Four

Frankie Lopez mounts the little stage at the back of the dining room. He takes the microphone from its stand, moves to the center like an experienced stand-up performer and addresses the crowd.

"Attention friends," he says calmly. "You all heard the announcement from the public address system. Apparently, there has been a misunderstanding between our party planners and the United States Marine Corps."

Laughter buzzes through the crowd, but there are also mumbles of concern.

"There's no real problem, amigos," continues Lopez. "I just spoke to the Marine Commander, and he's contacting Washington for some clarification."

"Why didn't you just invite them to the party?" one of the wedding guests shouts out.

"I did, but apparently, the Marines need approval from the President before they can party."

"Doesn't sound like the Marines I was a part of," shouts someone else.

"But you were in the Mexican Marines, Ricardo," Lopez answers. "And we know that Mexican Marines have never needed permission to party."

Everyone laughs at that including Lopez.

"Now, if you'll just relax," he adds, "I'm sure this little incident will be over in a few minutes. In the meantime, let's have some music. I think it's time for me to have a dance with the most beautiful woman here... my daughter, the bride."


As the musicians make their way onto the stage, and Frankie Lopez heads down to meet his daughter in the middle of the dance floor, Maria's cell phone rings.

Maria answers and then she frowns. It's her sister. And Claudia seems very concerned.

"Maria! Antonio and the strike force and I are at the Alamo. Where are you?"

"Why, we are at the Alamo too. And the food is wonderful."

"There's no food here, sis," Claudia answers. "Are you sure you are in the right place?"

"The Alamo Taqueria," says Maria. "But I think there's some trouble. The US Marines are here, and they are threatening to arrest everyone."

"WHAT? That's crazy," says Claudia. She has now switched her phone to SPEAKER, and everyone can hear. "Why do they think we'd want to capture a taqueria?"

"Los Tacos son sobrosisimos!" shouts Nacho who can't help but overhear the conversation. "And the press is here too. Some are covering the wedding of Frankie Lopez's daughter. But others want to report on the confrontation between the Marines and Claudia's Army."

"But Claudia's Army isn't even there. Or here. They are at the border creating a diversion."

"Well," answers Nacho, "apparently somebody told somebody about the invasion and said that you were going to seize the Alamo Taqueria.

"CNN is here, so is FOX News, ABC, NBC, and CBS, the Washington Post, the New York Times, and the Kankakee Daily Journal."

"Kankakee?"

"I guess they have a very active Hispanic community and are very interested in the fate of Claudia and her army."

"But who told them that we were going to seize a taqueria?" asks Claudia.

"Oh, no!" Antonio suddenly whispers to Claudia. "It was Tío Rafael,"

"What?" she asks as she pulls away from the phone.

"Tío Rafael told me that an American spy came to see him," Antonio says. "He recognized what she was, didn't want to give away our real plans, so he told her that we were planning to seize the Alamo Taqueria. I thought it was clever misinformation."

"Misinformation that has come back to bite us in the ass," adds Padre Carlos.

Claudia looks up. Everyone clusters around her and her phone now, even the Padre, even Linda the cashier.

"The Marines are calling Washington for clarification on how to handle the invaders," says Maria. "If you're really after publicity you'd better get over here now, Claudia."

Linda realizes that the events may be live on television and she rushes over to the small TV behind the cash register and switches it on.


A nighttime image of the Alamo Taqueria fills the screen. The multicolored lights flash the name boldly as a voice-over announcer says, "As you may be aware, a group of illegal aliens has taken over one of Texas's most famous restaurants, the Alamo Taqueria. A few minutes ago, one of our reporters, Ginger Mccloskey spoke to two of the combatants. Here's that interview."

The camera zooms in to reveal a redheaded news reporter standing near the entrance to the Taqueria. She motions for one of her colleagues to bring in an interviewee, and reluctantly Nacho walks up to her. Britney stands beside him, holding his arm, looking up at him in adoration.

"Could I have your name Sir?" Ginger asks.

"Francisco Alfredo Gonzales Gonzales Gonzales. But you can call me Nacho."

"Okay, Mr. Nacho," Ginger says. "Tell us... what are your intentions?"

"I claim this historic site in the name of the good people of Mexico."

"But it's fully within the borders of the United States of America."

"Yes, it is. I claim it anyway."

"And it's not a historic site; it's a taqueria."

"Well, I still claim it. The food is fabulous."

"You heard it here first, folks." Ginger says directly into the camera and to the audience. Then she turns to Britney.

"And what about you, miss?"

"I'm a singer at The Lone Coyote Bar in Mesa Texas... appearing Monday Wednesday and Friday nights from eight to midnight. Our group is called The Screaming Cowgirls."

"Appropriate name for a girl band, but what's your involvement with this group?"

"I fully support this handsome hombre."

"But you're not Mexican?"

"After all the enchiladas I've eaten tonight I probably am."

"There you have it. This is Ginger Mccloskey reporting live from the Alamo Taqueria in Mole Texas. Now back to our studios in New York."

At the network's studios, Anchorman Wolfe Trappe continues the report. "Reliable sources tell us that only two days ago,

President Drivel received an intelligence report telling him that, while Mexican troops continue to mass at the Mexican/American border, a small strike force from the same unit would soon set out to seize the Alamo Taqueria.

"Ginger," Wolf asks. "Do you have any information about Frankie Lopez's role in all of this?"

"I haven't been able to talk to him, Wolfe. Apparently, he's still dancing with his daughter."

"Not surprising," says Wolfe.

"I'll get to him as soon as I can."

Thank you, Ginger."

#

Inside the gift shop at the Alamo, Antonio and Claudia are flabbergasted.

"Somethin' just seems wrong with all this," says Linda as she watches Claudia and her strike force listen to the news report.

"We'd better get over to that Taqueria, Mija," says Antonio.

"I guess you're right," Claudia answers. And soon she, Antonio, Padre Carlos, and the others rush out to their little Chevy van.

"Hey, wait just one minute," moans Padre Carlos, "We forgot the flag."

"Leave it," says Antonio, "Let's remind the good people of Texas that we've been here."

"No way," snaps the priest. "It's the only flag we brought."

"Wait! What?" asks Antonio. "Who was in charge of bringing the flag?"

Padre Carlos blushes. "Tía Lucinda, I wanted to give her a chance to be part of the operation."

Antonio rolls his eyes. "So you left something important to a senile old woman?"

The priest nods.

"War is perhaps not the time to be so damn Christian, Padre."

"It's the VERY BEST time," answers the Priest proudly. "Anyway, do we really need the flag?"

"We should raise it proudly over this so-called Taqueria," grumbles Antonio.

Claudia is getting tired of the bickering, so she makes a command decision.

"The flag of Mexico should fly at the site of our real conquest," she says, "not as a sign of where we stopped along the way."

"I'll get it," says Antonio, and he rushes up onto the wall, retrieves the flag, returns to the van, hands the flag to the priest, and climbs in. Then, still bickering, the little strike force drives off into the night to encounter the Best Tacos in Texas and the United States Marines Corps.

# Chapter Thirty-Five

"What the hell is this," shouts Hector Oliva Junior, the Prince of Beans. His tank has just begun its daily patrol of the US Mexican Border. But now he orders the driver to stop and then jumps up out of the turret and stands watching as an entire contingent of the real Mexican army marches in between his tank and the border.

"Get down from there," a voice from a bullhorn calls to him, and Junior jumps down and watches as three soldiers march up to him.

"Just what are you doing, son?" asks the commander, General Suárez.

"Patrolling the border, trying to throw a little scare into these Gringo mercenaries."

"Believe me, they're seasoned soldiers; they've seen plenty of tanks," says Suárez. "Now, we are going to take up a position between your so-called Army and the Americans. We don't want anyone to provoke anyone and cause an international incident."

"I thought you said these were seasoned soldiers," says Junior. Suddenly one of the two men flanking the commander drops a heavy hand onto the kid's shoulder.

"You're speaking to a general in the Mexican Army, kid. Show some respect."

Junior looks terrified for a moment, but the General quiets his adjutant.

"At ease, Vargas," he says then turns back to the kid. "It's not the seasoned soldiers I'm worried about, son. It's those damn vigilantes. They'd just love to get something started, love to have a reason to knock off some of Claudia's Army. Now, just roll that tank back into camp while I have a word with Commander Don Juan. He's a fine soldier and was once under my command."

"Yeah, okay," says the kid, and again the big hand of Adjutant Vargas falls onto his soldier. "I mean, yes sir," the kid adds.


No more than a few football fields away, just beyond the American military command led by General Bradley Oldman, nearly a hundred vigilantes mass in their pick up trucks and vans. Many also have motorbikes, and they take turns dragging back and forth behind the protective ranks of the US National Guard. Perhaps more importantly, the guard has cordoned off a huge group of protestors calling themselves, "The Friends of Claudia." They are a mix of Mexican Americans and white middle class supporters from all over the United States. They carry signs many of which have a stenciled silhouette of a warrior woman in western gear and a sombrero. Feminist contingents within the ranks carry signs that simply say, "WE SUPPORT YOU, SISTER CLAUDIA!" Other signs read, "YOU GO GIRL," and "BRING DOWN THIS WALL." Two lanky cowboys from who-knows-where hold up the biggest sign of all reading "WHY CAN'T WE BE FRIENDS," while still others hold up placards that have a phrase which has become familiar to people worldwide: "SHRIVEL DRIVEL."

General Oldman turns to his adjutant. "Never saw anything like this in my life. Did you, Lieutenant?"

"No sir, not really," says Mona Esposito.

"You think the Mexican Army can help control Claudia and her gang?"

"Let's hope so," she sighs.


Now general Suárez sits across the table from Don Juan and Tío Rafael (who represents Claudia and Antonio).

"So you're not really going to invade?"

"That's right general," answers Rafael.

"This is just a diversion," adds Don Juan.

"Hell of an expensive diversion," says Suárez. "Our part of this little exercise is costing the Mexican Government about ten million pesos."

Rafael sighs. "Pardon my saying so, commander, but no one asked for your protection."

Suárez eyes Don Juan who merely shrugs as much as to say, "See what I have to put up with."

"Why are you helping these locos?" Suárez asks Don Juan.

"Hundreds of people are joining them every day," he answers. "El Rey del Frijol has given them money and arms and a tank. I figured some training is better than no training at all."

Suárez nods then turns back to Rafael, "But your real target is...."

"The Alamo, of course," says the old man. "Why, when I rode with Pancho Villa..."

"Damn," says Suárez cutting him off immediately. "That should sit well with the gringos. You want to capture one of their national shrines... *the* national shrine of the state of Texas... as a publicity stunt."

Rafael suddenly pounds the table violently. "We have to do it, and we can. Sí, Sí Puede."

"Yeah, right," sighs Suárez. "And you really agree with this nonsense, Juan?"

"You know the story, right, general?" asks the soldier.

"I'm not sure."

"Why don't you tell him from the beginning, Tío."

And so Rafael retells Claudia's story from Tío Joaquín's injury, but with greater emphasis in his own role in solidifying the cause, and then adding several "Sí, Sí Puedes" for emphasis.

Meanwhile General Oldman and Lieutenant Esposito watch with great concern as Mexican National Troops line up on the opposite side of the border.

Behind General Oldman, the US National Guard stands ready to strike. Even further back, rows upon rows of Texas Vigilantes sit on the backs of hundreds of Pick-up trucks with their rifles poised. But there are almost as many protestors supporting the Mexican cause. The soldiers on either side are silent. Behind the Mexican army, Junior's tank rumbles, and the thousands of Mexican citizen-soldiers who have joined Claudia's Army stand prepared for action.

# Chapter Thirty-Six

Nacho stands atop of the wall of the Alamo Taqueria surveying the contingents of US Marines, Texas Vigilantes and Pro Claudia Protestors.

Antonio climbs up the steps and stands beside Nacho on the wall. He too takes in the sight and seems very surprised. Nacho suddenly notices him and turns.

"Do I know you?" he asks. "Are you part of the army?"

"Claudia's Army," answers Antonio. "I'm her partner in the enterprise."

"Claudia's here?"

"Oh yeah. We came in as the wedding guests were leaving. Snuck in through the crowd."

Nacho nods. "The US Marines finally got an okay to let the wedding guests leave the Taqueria without being shot."

Antonio looks on in disbelief.

"Even then it wasn't that easy," says Nacho. "In the end, the Rosas family had to agree to provide free tacos to all the Marines. They rolled out a little taco truck with a big picture of Adelita on the side."

Antonio nods, "The heroine of so many folk tales, the Joan of Arc of Mexico." He chuckles to himself, "The Claudia of her time."

Nacho nods and smiles. "I love that girl."

"So do I," adds Antonio.

"Frankie Lopez wanted to stay," says Nacho, "but the Marines insisted that he leave with his guests."

"Makes sense. America has to protect her TV stars."


Suddenly, the men are distracted by the whop, whop, whop of an enormous American helicopter that slowly circles the Taqueria and then lands directly between the Marines and the restaurant. The Chopper bears the seal of the President of the United States.

"We have important visitors," says Antonio. And they do. The door to the chopper slides back, and a hoard of secret service agents jump through the billowing dust. In another moment so does Daniel Drivel.

Following Drivel is a tall, dark and yes, handsome man.

"El Presidente," says Nacho and he salutes.

It's Ricardo de la Palma Alta, the President of Mexico. He and Drivel rush away from the chopper followed by an entire entourage including a hooded Mexican Monk (part of de la Palma's retinue) a malevolent-looking anti-immigration Senator, and Appassionata Sanchez the spy who rested the information about the taqueria from Tío Rafael. Today, apparently, she's using her skills and knowledge as a hostage negotiator.

She carries a bullhorn. And, as soon as the chopper engines quiet completely, she raises the horn, turns toward the taqueria, and calls:

"The presidents of both our countries would like to speak to the leaders of Claudia's Army."

"Would that be you and Claudia?" asks Nacho.

"I'm afraid so," says Antonio.

"Sad."

"Sad?"

"I was hoping it could be me too. I'm starting to enjoy the fact that Claudia has an army."

Antonio smiles at the big man. Then he turns to the Presidential party, cups his hands and calls: "Can you assure our safety?"

"Listen Chico..." Drivel shouts, but Appassionata cuts him off. "Young man, we are surrounded by cameras and reporters from all over the world. I can assure you that no one would dare shoot you with the whole world watching."

The wind picks up for a moment. It scatters dust into the eyes of the presidents and their entourage, but Antonio's words rise above it.

"WE ARE COMING."

Antonio starts toward the stairs and then he turns to Nacho.

"Come along," he says. "And bring your guitar."

Nacho grabs his old friend, slings it over his shoulder and starts down the stairs behind Antonio. On the way out of the restaurant, Claudia steps in beside them.

"Stay back," says Antonio as he tries to restrain her. "I don't want to risk your life too."

"But Antonio, this is my army," she says with a smile. "Or have you forgotten?"

The young man chuckles, and Claudia leads the way out through the great doors.


Soon Claudia, Antonio, and Nacho approach the President's party. Nacho is carrying another white flag made from a souvenir Alamo Taqueria t-shirt. It hangs rather proudly from the very last of the plastic souvenir swords in the gift shop. But before they can reach the heads of state, several Secret Service agents stop the trio.

"Surrender your weapons," demands a man in a black suit and tie and dark glasses.

"None here," answers Antonio holding up his hands.

"As you wish, gentlemen," says Claudia, and she gracefully removes the bandoliers that crisscross her chest; then she pulls two large pistols out of her belt and hands them over.

"I'm clean," says Nacho.

"That looks like a sword to me," answers the Secret Service Man and he pulls a gun and pushes it right into Nacho's nose. "We're not fucking around here, fat man."

And so Nacho meekly presents his sword and the souvenir T-shirt.

"Now you may proceed," the agent says, and the three continue to walk the short distance to the world leaders.

As they approach they can see that the two politicos are bickering, but when Claudia, Antonio, and Nacho arrive, the American President stops and addresses them.

"Just what the hell do you think you're doing?" he asks, "seizing the best taqueria in Texas?"

"Have you eaten here?" asks Nacho, "the food es fantástico."

"Maybe," Drivel responds, "but this is ridiculous. It's an act of war. We have the place surrounded. You can see all the Marines. And let me add that they are very fine Marines, excellent Marines, fully capable of destroying you with fire and fury."

"To do that," Claudia answers with a smug smile, "You'll have to destroy a wonderful restaurant, as well as the owners and their staff."

"I don't care," answers Drivel. "We are prepared to take whatever action is necessary to maintain our sovereignty."

Nacho sighs. "If we knew you were going to do that we would have recaptured the real Alamo."

Now anti-immigration Senator Bobby Joe Connelly speaks up. "Don't you crazy Mexicans know that the Alamo is hallowed ground? Great American heroes gave their lives on that holy spot: Jim Bowie, William B. Travis, Davy Crockett."

"And hundreds of great Mexican heroes gave their lives there as well," counters Nacho, "including my great-great uncle Hector, 'Nacho,' Cortez Fernando Garcia Garcia Garcia."

"Three Garcias," mumbles Drivel, "Outrageous!"

"This is a shameful day for our country," says Mexican President Ricardo de la Palma Alta. "Your actions make all our people look foolish, and they threaten the lives and the security of millions on both sides of..."

"Cut the bullshit, Ricardo," interrupts Drivel. "These assholes attempted to seize the most sacred shrine in the great state of Texas. They missed their mark and got an incredible Taqueria instead. But the crime was in their intentions. I believe they deserve to die."

Mexican Presidente de la Palma Alta gasps. "These heroes do not deserve to die," he says. "They are guilty of no other crime than perhaps... *tourism.*"

"Don't horseshit me, Ricardo, I'm sendin' these heroes of yours to Guantanamo. I intend to make examples of them all."

And now he turns to Claudia. "Pardon my French Miss, but you lousy Mexicans are going to have to learn that..."

"Lousy Mexicans?" de la Palma Alta shouts, "Sir, let me remind you that you are speaking to the leader of millions of lousy Mexicans, as you call us. I want you to know that Claudia and I have a million-man/woman army poised on your border, and if I give the command they will surge forward and support these... these... *heroes!*"

"Gentlemen, please!" chides Negotiator Appassionata Sanchez.

"Just shut up, Appassionata," says Drivel then he turns back to the President of Mexico.

"Now pay attention, Ricardo, you have to think about this realistically. I'm a realist. And I have to tell you that you are flirting with fire and fury, and maybe even things worse than that... much worse. I'm the commander and chief of the greatest army in the world, and all I have to do is issue a simple order... that's all I have to do... and hundreds of atom bombs will rain down on you and your taco-eating country and blow you all to smithereens!"

"You think you are the only ones with nuclear weapons?" shouts de la Palma Alta. "We have an enormous nuclear stockpile that we've been building for years."

"That's impossible!" answers Drivel. "I'm the President of the United States, and I would know about it if you did. I have the greatest intelligence in the world. Isn't that right Ms. Sanchez?"

Appassionata looks away for a moment then turns to the Commander and Chief. "Absolutely, Sir. Without a doubt."

"Besides," Drivel continues, "Where would you get all those nukes?"

"You think Iran is the only country with a covert nuclear weapons program?"

"Are you threatening America with nuclear war?"

"Is that what you want, Señor Presidente, because Mexico is fully capable of launching weapons of mass destruction."

"And just what are those weapons, Ricardo? Flying tacos with extra spicy sauce? Enchiladas al diablo?"

"That sounds delicious," sighs Nacho.

"But the North won't be that lucky," adds de la Palma Alta.

Both men pause for a moment to catch their breath, and now they stand with clenched fists and red faces, grimacing at each other. And suddenly they are caught in a downpour. Rain floods onto both of them, but only them.

Claudia glances up and sees that familiar watery triangle floating in the air above the two men. "ATP, Atmospheric Triangular Phenomena," she sighs. "Perhaps it has a spiritual element."

Now, the two men look up in shock and see it too. They try to run back to the protection of the helicopter, but the cloudburst follows them dumping rain as they go. When they split apart the triangle splits in two and follows each of them separately.

Claudia is laughing, not spitefully, not cruelly, just honestly. The sound is like a song or the sweetest whisper of the wind or a young woman's gentle laughter. Because that's what it is.

"You silly men," Claudia shouts. "No wonder our countries can't get along, when our leaders act like little children caught in a sudden rainstorm, blaming each other for everything."

The presidents turn toward her, cock their heads as though the downpour has perhaps had some transformative effect on their thinking. And just like that, the rain stops, and the triangles disappear. But now, there's the sharp snap of a pistol shot.

Drivel freezes. "What was that, someone trying to shoot me?"

The secret service men draw their guns and spin toward the crowd, others run back to the President. "Time to go sir," says the lead agent.

"No friends. It's okay," says President de la Palma Alta. "It's just someone shooting off firecrackers in celebration. It's a Mexican custom, happens every time we're really happy."

"I don't like it, sir," says the secret service guy. "We'd better go."

"But we finally have a chance to talk," says Antonio, "Let's be brave enough to take it."

"Please, Mr. President," adds Claudia.

# Chapter Thirty-Seven

"Stranger! Hey, Lone Stranger, wake up."

Clayton Bailey pops his eyes open and stares into the lovely face of Moonglow O'Riley.

"Where am I," he mumbles.

"At the *Friends of Mexico* camp just outside the Alamo Taqueria, silly," she answers. "The President of the United States is here, so's the President of Mexico."

Bailey groans. His head feels like it's full of alfalfa, and he sure doesn't care about the President of Mexico.

"Remind me never to taste that loco weed again," he sighs and rolls away from her.

"Come on, Lone," whispers Moonglow. "SHE's here too."

"Who's she," Bailey asks without turning back to the smiley young woman.

"Claudia, Masked Man, the leader of Claudia's Army. She's here with some guy named Antonio..."

"Who cares?"

"And another guy named Nacho."

Bailey jumps up in bed as though he's heard a bugle call. He turns to Moonglow, and his eyes suddenly sparkle.

"Nacho?" he asks. "A big guy, carries a guitar on his back. Shuffles when he walks? Always says Ka-BLAM?"

"That's him," says Moonglow. "He's talkin' to the president right now. Come on; let's cheer em on. Let the president know how much we admire Claudia and her people."

Bailey is up on his feet, wide-awake and pulling on his boots. He straightens his shirt, adjusts his mask, straps on his guns.

Moonglow looks concerned for a moment and then she smiles. "Gonna shoot up into the air as a sign of support?" Her voice is full of admiration.

"What?" asks Bailey without even looking at her, "Oh yeah. Sure. That's exactly what I intend to do."

"But is it safe?" asks Moonglow. "They probably won't let you get away with it, but come on, hurry. The guys are holding a spot for us right up front, near the action."

"That's just where I want to be," growls Bailey. "So's I can make a little *action* of my own."


Moments later, Moonglow and Bailey are standing at the very front of a troop of Claudia's supporters who have a ringside view of the presidential conversation. A hundred yards to their right, the presidential party stands talking to the Mexican heroes: Claudia, Antonio, and Nacho. About ten yards closer to the building a half dozen Secret Service Agents study the crowed, arms crossed, hands on hips, threatening expressions on their faces.

A few yards closer still to the Taqueria and almost in front of Moonglow and her friends, Nick, Maria, Juanito, and Britney stand watching the conversation. The crowd rumbles noisily, and firecrackers continue to be thrown out into the plaza. They pop and sizzle in the morning sunshine.

"There's the good ol boy who started it all," grumbles Bailey when he sees Nick, "bringing them vermin onto his ranch, takin care a them like they was real people... givin' his sister to one a them. You bastard, Fleming!"

"Ka-Blam, ka-Blam," says Nacho giving the presidents his best imitation of the popular explosives.

"Yeah, I got it," says Drivel.

And then: BANG! BANG!

Drivel looks annoyed, "More damn firecrackers," he says. But then there's a scream.

"Oh God, no! Please Jesus," shouts Maria as she sees Nick fall.

Bailey quickly fades back into the crowd before anyone realizes that the sounds were gunshots and not fireworks. Maria pulls Nick to her and cradles him in her arms.

"Holy smoke," says Drivel. "She's hugging that white guy."

"Romeo and Juliet, Señor," says Nacho, and he begins to sob. But then he sees Nick leaning on Maria as she helps him to his feet.

"Just grazed me," Nick says, though he winces and Maria can see blood smeared across his shirt. Still, he takes off his hat and waves at the crowd. Everyone cheers, even Ricardo de la Palma Alta, even Daniel Drivel.

The couple and the little boy hobble toward the group of negotiators, but of course the secret service men stop them for a security inspection.

Still, Nacho seizes the moment.

"Did you see that," he cries. "For just one second everyone stopped hating and fighting and threatening to blow this planet to smithereens.

"And why? Because of LOVE, amigos, that's why."

Other members of the party step back. News cameramen and women move in as he speaks.

"Why can't we just remember that," Claudia says suddenly stepping forward and addressing the presidents and the media. "Can't we just stop thinking of ourselves for once, stop wanting everything we see, stop being so greedy? Just wake up to the love around us, enjoy that, and learn to share it."

Antonio nods proudly as he hears her words.

"Plus," Claudia continues as she turns to the presidents and addresses them almost directly, "We need to add one more thing to our loving relationships. We must *share power* too so all of us can advance."

All over the world TV sets show Nacho and Claudia's impassioned plea for love, understanding, and equality. Women sob, children nod knowingly. Men blink back tears. Yes, some haters flip off their sets any way they can. Still, the message is heard.

# Chapter Thirty-Eight

"You worthless pile of garbage!"

Clayton Bailey suddenly bursts from the crowd and steps right up to Nacho before the rabid security men can gun him down.

"Hold on! Hold on," says Drivel raising his small hands to stop the advance of the Secret Service. "Just who is this masked man?"

"It ain't the Lone Ranger!" says Nacho.

"Of course, not," says Drivel, "he's wearing baby blue, not powder blue."

"Perceptive," Nacho adds.

"Listen," Bailey grunts to the big man. "You've stolen my girl, corrupted her soul with spicy food and filled her head with your refried ideas. Now it's time for revenge."

There's a deafening series of clicks as every gun in the Secret Service and the US military cocks and points directly at Bailey.

The masked man looks around, and then he smiles bitterly. "I have nothing to live for," he tells the president, "except to put a silver bullet into the heart of this stupid nacho-man."

"No! Wait!" Claudia shouts. But it's too late. Bailey pulls the trigger and shoots. But at the last minute, the hooded monk from de la Palma's entourage jumps in front of Nacho and takes the bullet for him. Then the monk staggers backward and falls to the ground.

Almost in slow motion, Nacho roars, "El Ka-BLAM!" as he jerks the guitar from behind his back, spins like a ninja warrior, and clubs Bailey right on the head.

Several Secret Service men now rush forward and grab the fallen assassin. The crowd in front of the fallen monk suddenly clears. They help him to his feet. He's standing again, ripping off his shirt, and showing the bulletproof vest that saved him.

"See, Padre," says President Drivel, "I told you we all needed to be prepared for an attack when we headed out here."

"But who is he," asks Nacho. "Who saved me?"

The monk pulls back his cowl, and smiles sheepishly out at them.

"Oh my God," gasps Claudia.

"It can't be," says Nacho and he drops his guitar with a dissident SPROING!

"Chato?" says Maria as she rushes to the man. She stares at him and he at her.

"I felt I had to come back and help you," he murmurs. "I've regretted what happened between us all my life. I'm even sorry for the trouble I caused that fat kid over there."

Maria laughs through her tears.

Nacho laughs too, " No problem man," he says. "After all, you did give me... Ka–BLAM."

Maria hugs Chato, "thank you father," she says and then she walks slowly back to Nick. She looks up at him wondering for a moment if he wants her to explain, but he shakes his head.

"It's okay," he whispers. Then he wipes away her tears and kisses her cheek. "Some other time."


Meanwhile, the Secret Service men have subdued Bailey and hold him pinned to the ground, and yet he is still jerking around like a lunatic. They roll their eyes, as does Nacho who turns back to the cameras and continues unabated.

"Friends, why must we keep on fighting? Can't we follow the example of this wonderful priest who turned from a bully to a hero to save my life? Can't we live for love and brotherhood?"

President Drivel shrugs, nods, raises one of his small hands to make a point, but just then his stomach begins to rumble. He looks around desperately. "Isn't there ANYTHING we can get to eat around here?"

He sees vigilantes, supporters of Claudia's Army, the Marines, and even the secret service agents looking hungry as hell.

"Ladies and gentlemen," says Nacho, "we are standing in front of the restaurant that sells The Best Tacos in Texas."

"Amen," says Chato, and the president nods his approval.

"So why don't we just agree to learn to live together and do what we all do best?"

"And just what is that?" asks Drivel.

"Come on," says Nacho. "Don't you know?"

"Invade the greatest country on earth, steal our jobs and our health care benefits?" says Drivel.

Nacho looks at Claudia, Antonio, Maria, and Nick and then he raises his hands to the skies. "Madre de Dios! Will he never understand?" he shouts, but somehow he restrains himself.

"Forgive me, Mr. President. Perhaps I did not make myself clear. What do we Mexicans do best, that I'm sure your people do very well also?"

"Elect strong, caring leaders such as myself and Mr. de la Palma Alta here?"

"Yeah, right," says Claudia rolling her eyes.

"No way, Jose," says Antonio.

Nacho just shakes his head and turns to Britney. "Come on Sweetness. Say it with me."

The singing cowgirl's eyes light up and she and Nacho shout together:

**"FIESTA!!"**

Suddenly, the doors to the Taqueria burst open and a Mariachi band emerges. On either side of the lead trumpeter are women dressed in bright red Mexican party dresses and singing their hearts out.

Spontaneous cheers arise from the Marines, the Secret Service, and the President of Mexico.

"Well, why didn't you say so," says Drivel as he begins clapping to the music. "I finally get it."

Spy and hostage negotiator, Appassionata Sanchez, lunges forward and plants a passionate kiss on the president's lips.

"Young woman, isn't that a bit inappropriate?" asks Drivel.

Appassionata actually blushes.

"Perhaps he is a changed man," says Nacho.

Maria looks up sweetly at Nick, and he bends down and kisses her. Claudia reaches for Antonio pulls him to her and whispers, "I think somehow we have accomplished our mission." She gives him a very sweet kiss, and Antonio responds by sweeping her off her feet, dipping her almost to the ground, and kissing her with all the passion of a romantic hero from an old time movie.

Nacho runs up to Chato and throws his arms around him. They talk for a moment. "Pray for me, father," says Nacho. "And you for me," answers the one time bully.

Now, dozens of waiters swarm out of the taqueria carrying trays full of tacos and pitchers of beer and margaritas. The president grabs a taco and munches it happily.

De la Palma Alta grabs a gigantic burrito and takes a big bite.

Meanwhile, the waiters set up a great table for all the onlookers, the press, the vigilantes, the picketers and the protesters. They swarm together forming a neat but completely integrated line chatting amiably as they wait for their serving.

"Hey look at this," calls reporter Ginger Mccloskey. She points to a TV monitor that shows the US Mexican Border where a parade of taco trucks rolls through the uncompleted section of the wall and begins serving tacos and enchiladas to the National Guard Troops, Claudia's Army, the Mexican Army, the vigilantes, and the protestors.

"My goodness, they're serving everyone," says Drivel. "Where did those trucks come from?"

"I took a chance," says Miguel Rosas who arrived with the Mariachis. "When things started really getting tense, I decided that the best solution, as always, is to start serving *really good food.*"

"It makes us strong," adds Claudia.

"It unites us," says de La Palma Alta.

"Since the US Marines wouldn't let my employees go home," Rosas continues, "I decided to put them to work. We started cooking and cooking and cooking.

"Then, under cover of darkness..."

Nacho manages to strum a dramatic chord on what's left of his guitar, and the mariachis pick up the note and hold it.

*"... I sent out my taco trucks,*
*As many as I could.*
*I asked them to go to the border*
*And serve everyone equally:*
*Soldiers on every side,*
*Vigilantes, protestors,*
*Even the guy in the tank."*

215

A shot of Hector Oliva Junior just happens to fill the TV screen at that moment. He has a paper plate, and he's ramming forkfuls of enchilada into his mouth. He gives the camera a big thumbs up.

"I wasn't sure there would be enough food," says Miguel, "but almost miraculously the tortillas and beans and carnitas just seemed to multiply."

"It's a miracle," says Maria.

"But perhaps it's been done before," adds Antonio.

"Only this time with better food," laughs Nacho.

"Or not," whispers Chato.


The mingling, the partying and music and eating and drinking continue.

"I haven't had this much fun in years," says Drivel. "We need to do this more often, Ricardo."

De la Palma Alta nods in agreement. "Perhaps a joint national holiday," he suggests.

"Great idea," answers Drivel. "We can meet every year at the border and celebrate our friendship."


Meanwhile, on the huge TV screen, Newsman Wolfe Trappe is at the border and has cornered the American Commander General Bradley Oldman. At this point, vigilantes are mixing with protestors and members of all the different armies, and people's goals are almost indistinguishable.

"Tell me, Commander," says Wolfe, "It looks like people from all sides are milling around everywhere, how are you going to restore order. How are you going to make sure everyone ends up on the right side of the border?"

Oldman crams an entire taco into his mouth, chews on it for a moment, takes a swig of cervesa, shrugs, and merely asks, *"What friggin' border?"*

As Nacho and the others stand watching the newsfeed, he puts his arm around his singing cowgirl and pulls her to him. "Imagine those words coming from an American military commander, Beautiful," he whispers to Britney. "'Qué Frontera?' What an interesting question."

Then the mariachis crash in with more music, and the party continues.

THE END

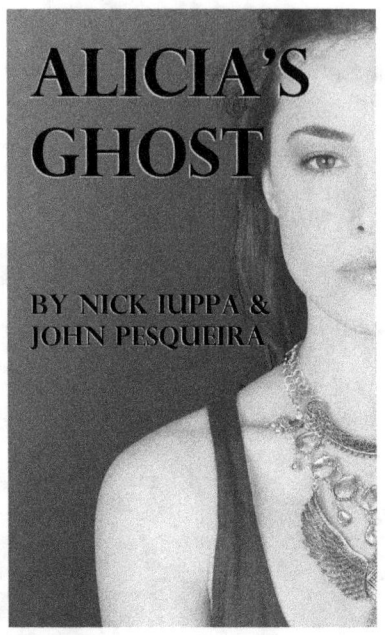

# Bonus Chapter

Available NOW
from Nick Iuppa and John Pesqueira

## The Complete Carlos Mann Trilogy

Love, Obsession, Murder, Mexico, Mannequins,
Rattlesnakes, Drug Lords, Chinatown, Ghosts...
And the World's Most Haunting Heroine

# BOOK ONE
## ALICIA'S GHOST

The astoundingly beautiful Alicia has ended her modeling career in Mexico City, married the love of her life, helped pay his way through college, settled into a comfortable existence in Los Altos California, and now she's dead... MURDERED. Her husband, Professor Carlos Mann, has wrapped himself in an obsessive-compulsive disorder to hide from that fact. But when Amy Joy, one of Carlos's students, is sold into slavery by a Chinese mob that traffics in Asian girls, Alicia returns with a vengeance.

Can Alicia save her man, foil the human traffickers, and destroy her murderer? Overwhelming supernatural forces stand against her. But that just makes her stronger!

Told in the voices of Carlos and Alicia Mann, Alicia's Ghost is a funny, imaginative and thrilling ride through the human and spirit worlds of Mexico and the American Southwest.

*Read on for a preview of the adventures of Carlos and Alicia.*

# Chapter 1
# Carlos Mann

Alicia and I are walking along the beach in San Lucero, Mexico. Endless sand, endless condos, endless kids running up to us trying to sell toys and tacos and woodcarvings of turtles and starfish.

Alicia is wearing a bikini so skimpy I'm embarrassed. I'm also proud and excited. She looks lovingly at me, blessing me with the brightness of her smile and those eyes that won't stop sparkling.

Two old women approach us from the other direction. They are dressed in flowing summer wraps. They hobble through the wet sand and stare at us in disapproval. Alicia is hanging on me, kissing me, and giggling. One arm is around my neck; she's bending forward. Her breasts struggle to jump out of her bikini. Her legs step across mine as though we're dancing.

To the old women we're naughty children. And sometimes Alicia looks like she's about fifteen. To me, she's the little girl I grew up with, my best bud, my lover, and my fiancée. She's actually making it possible for me to attend graduate school at Leland University in the United States.

She flashes her engagement ring at the old women, but they still sneer and call her "Puta!"

She sticks her tongue out at them and crosses her eyes. Then she missteps, trips over my legs, and falls pulling me down on top of her. She rolls us both over and straddles me.

220

The old women are disgusted. They snap their heads in the other direction and struggle on up the beach toward a bright orange taqueria whose canopy promises margaritas and shade from the Mexican sun.

"Take me with you tomorrow, mi amor," Alicia says, "... to the University. Take me."

I smile. I can't say no. But I have to.

"We're just not ready to move to the United States together." I say.

She scrunches up her face like a spoiled five-year-old.

"You know I'll send for you as soon as I have things set up."

"That won't be soon enough," she sighs. Suddenly her voice starts fading, becoming very distant.

"It's just a few months away."

"NO!" She sounds desperate.

"Why?" I ask.

"BECAUSE I'M ALREADY *DEAD!*"


Gashes suddenly cut across Alicia's chest and arms; a deep wound opens on her throat. Her legs are shredded. She rolls from me ... a wretched corpse!

"Alicia!" I jump to my feet and go to her, looking down at her in the sand. Her hand reaches up to me as blood pours down her arm. It fills her eyes, pools in her hair, spills over her lips. "Mi amor!" Her words are little more than a whisper.

The sand now fades into the soft carpet of our apartment in Los Altos, California. But Alicia is still dead, more dead *here* because this is where I found her, the way I found her, slashed and murdered.

"I love you," she moans as her image begins to fade. "I will always love you. Love me forever."

I jump bolt upright in bed, awakening from another terrible dream. My t-shirt is soaked front and back. The sheets are dripping with perspiration. The pillows look like a swamp. But the ghostly moans still ring in the air: "Love me forever."

I turn to Alicia's side of the bed. No one is there. No one has been there for three years. Alicia is really dead, really murdered. But I've been true to her. I still love her.

Too bad she doesn't believe me.

# About the Authors

*Nick Iuppa began his career as an apprentice writer with famed Bugs Bunny/Road Runner animator Chuck Jones and children's author Dr. Seuss. He later became a staff writer for the* Wonderful World of Disney. *As VP Creative Director for Paramount Pictures, Nick did experimental work in interactive television and story-based simulations. He is the author of seven novels,* Management by Guilt *(Fawcett Books 1984—a Fortune Book Club selection) and eight technical books on interactive media. He lives in Northern California with his wife, Ginny. For more about Nick, visit www.nickiuppa.com.*

*John Pesqueira's studies at the University of Arizona, Columbia, and Stanford prepared him for an impressive career in media design and development. His passion for the visual arts and popular culture continue to inform his creative efforts and still inspire his writing and photography. John grew up in the Sonoran desert and his love of the history, legends, and people of the American Southwest and Mexico remain a major focus of his work. John lives with his wife in Northern California.*

223

# Contact Us

We love hearing from our readers and learning what they like or don't like about our stories. We'd be very grateful if you would send us a quick e-mail and tell us what you think of *The Battle for the Alamo Taqueria*. We promise we'll answer personally and directly.

Please contact us at the link below to tell us what you think and let us thank you for reading our books.

Contact Nick & John at
dosmilagrospress@Gmail.com